Soldier with Benefits

A Steamy Action Adventure Romance

Shelley Munro

Munro Press

Soldier with Benefits

Print ISBN: 978-1-99-106326-7
Digital ISBN: 978-0-473-33035-4

Editor: Mary Moran

Cover: Kim Killion, The Killion Group, Inc.

Munro Press, New Zealand.

First Munro Press electronic publication August 2015

First Munro Press print publication April 2023

For Paul, the man who sees me faults and all but still loves me.

INTRODUCTION

JOANNA "MAC" MCGREGOR LOVES her father, and she'll do anything to keep him safe after Alzheimer's starts to steal his mind. That takes money, and Mac uses her only skills—those of soldiering—when she takes up a security contract to protect VIPs in Iraq. She doesn't have time for men, her last vacation fling in Fiji relegated as one perfect moment to hold close during the grim reality of war.

Soldier and protector, Louie Lithgow is tired of fighting—the constant danger—and has decided this is his last contract. He wants to retire, sink his savings into a place on the beach, and find the sexy Joanna, his holiday lover.

Mac's arrival in Iraq causes consternation. They've both been economical with the truth, but the attraction sizzling between them flares hot and bright. They embark on a clandestine affair—professional and confident during their high-danger day, passionate with the release of emotional stress during their torrid nights. One thing is clear—they have different goals, and the future is both murky and dangerous...if they survive their contracts.

Contains a military alpha male and a determined female soldier, melt-your-panties sex, friendship, and camaraderie, and...oh, more hot New Zealand romance.

Note to Readers

When I wrote *Innocent Next Door*, I thought it would be a standalone book, but Louie and Jake had other ideas and demanded they have their own stories. Now, Dillon and Josh are issuing bossy orders at me, too. I am determined they will get their comeuppance with feisty heroines who won't take their alpha tendencies too seriously. Watch this space!

Shelley

CHAPTER ONE

THE CHARTER FLIGHT FROM Jordan to Iraq was a short hop but plenty long enough for Joanna "Mac" McGregor to second-guess her decision to take up a contract in the security sector with Chesterton UK.

The wheels of the plane hit the runway, a solid thump before the pilot applied the brakes. Tension seeped into hands holding a fantasy paperback, turning her knuckles white. It wasn't just her. Even the guys at the back of the plane—the ones who had bantered their way through the entire journey and tried to tempt her into joining the Mile High Club—fell silent.

Mac stared out the window. She'd seen the stark reality of Baghdad firsthand when the plane circled the runway to land—the endless sand giving way to the greener city. Checkpoints. Security forces. Burned-out vehicles, buildings damaged by both allies' and insurgents' bombs.

Too late to change her mind and return to New Zealand now.

She'd gone through the lengthy interview process, answered all the questions about why a woman would want to undertake such a dangerous assignment and finally signed on the dotted line. After all, not much call for her skill set in an office, and she couldn't earn this sort of money doing anything else. Icy determination to succeed curled through her gut, squared her shoulders.

Mac disembarked with the rest of the security force, a few intrepid reporters and a camera crew, the initial blast of heat when she walked down the stairs sucking her lungs dry. Sweat broke out over her body and her shirt soon clung to her clammy skin. Something she'd become used to quickly.

After formalities, she waited with the other private security recruits—the new ones and the others who had signed on for a second or third tour. Like her, they were in it for the money, some for the adrenaline rush. Some of them would return home to family and friends. Some would die. Time would tell which camp she fell into.

The only route into the city, dubbed Route Irish by the Americans, was the most hazardous stretch of road in the world. Despite the fences on both sides, there were risky overpasses and numerous car bombs planted to snare the unwary. From the briefing, Mac knew they'd attempt to drive straight through any situation, be it bullets or bombs. Stopping wasn't an option.

Five minutes later, they pulled out in convoy, protected by security forces from New Zealand and the United Kingdom, their driver pausing to wait while a United States military convoy crossed the road ahead of them.

Overhead Mac watched two Black Hawk helicopters drawing fire, diverting it from the road. The entire time their vehicle remained in radio contact with others from the convoy. The drivers and guards constantly assessed risk, on the lookout for threats.

Mac stared out the window, gut jumping because she knew danger lurked around every corner. Signs at the checkpoint authorizing lethal force brought home the reality of her situation. If she found herself in the wrong place at the wrong time, she would die. No one left to look after her father then. She scowled at the thought and shoved it away.

Their convoy drove past the International zone, patrolled by the US military, the only part of the city considered relatively safe. They didn't stop, their destination the less-secure area where many private security forces and their clients lived.

The Red zone—her home for the next six months.

Mac climbed from the rear of the armored vehicle, grabbed her gear, and followed the other recruits into the main barrack-like building. All the domestic comforts, Mac thought, taking in the mismatched furniture, the clean but scuffed linoleum floor and the poster of a busty blonde hanging drunkenly on the far wall. She dumped her bags at her feet.

A tall, dark-haired man prowled through a doorway on her right and headed to the front of the room, his piercing brown eyes taking in the new arrivals. Mac's breath caught the instant she glimpsed his face, hurled back to the past.

Louie?

Shock drop-kicked her square in the gut. Why wasn't he at home in New Zealand? Only her military training kept her face impassive, the astonished gasp trapped inside her throat. Her training did nothing to halt the images flooding her mind, the memories of hard tattooed muscles beneath her questing fingers and the way it had felt each time his cock plunged between her legs.

Damn, Louie had lied to her.

His gaze slid over her and continued, but Mac knew by the slight widening of his eyes he'd recognized her. Probably dealing with the same stunned shock as her.

Baghdad wasn't exactly a place she'd expect to run into a former lover. Heck, she hadn't anticipated seeing Louie again at all. They'd been two people scratching an itch with no intention of taking their relationship further. Just good clean fun between like-minded adults relaxing on a tropical holiday.

Louie dispatched the new arrivals with military precision and soon only she remained, waiting for a room allocation.

"Joanna, what the hell are you doing here?" A tic pulsed in his jaw, highlighting his displeasure.

Mac scowled. "I'm here to do a job. Mac McGregor. I should be on your list."

Louie scanned his list and shoved it into the back pocket of his khaki trousers before stalking closer. "You told me you were a secretary."

Because she didn't talk about her job. Because she hated the inevitable questions. Because she'd wanted to forget the nightmare of war for the duration of her holiday.

Louie kept coming but Mac held her ground, refusing to let him intimidate her. Finally he halted, standing close enough for the heat emanating off his muscular body to bring another rush of memories. She drew a ragged breath, shoving aside the frisson of awareness.

Not gonna happen. This was work.

At almost six foot, she was tall, but he towered over her, forcing Mac to crane her neck to look him in the eye. "You told me you were a lawyer, not that we did much talking while we were in Fiji." She caught the flare of his nostrils, the slight narrowing of his eyes and knew Louie wasn't as unaffected as he pretended.

"You can't stay."

"I've signed a contract."

"You're a woman."

"Give the man a prize." Mac wanted to say a lot more but bit down on her tongue, figuring she'd better not cuss her new boss. The necessity to prove herself in the male-dominated occupation wore thin after a while. "I'm ex-army with ten years experience. I've worked in Afghanistan for six months. I'm good at my job or I wouldn't be in Iraq."

"It's dangerous. People die here." Louie's gaze drifted across her lips, settled for an instant before he backed up and glanced away.

"That's why I came. To help keep workers safe during the reconstruction process. I want to make a difference, and besides, this is the only way to make quick money." And boy did she need it.

"Your presence is going to be a problem."

Mac's mouth dropped open. Once she realized, she

slammed it shut so quickly her teeth clacked. "Oh yeah? Frightened you can't keep your hands off?"

He sure as hell hadn't called that a problem when they were in Fiji. Mac quivered inside, her breasts prickling when she remembered how it had been—the hot, urgent hunger between them. The sweet release of tension.

"This has nothing to do with sex. It's about how the men will feel working with a woman. It will divide their concentration."

"Bullshit," Mac snarled, sick of fighting the same old skirmish. She advanced on Louie, poking her finger at his chest to punctuate her words. "I'm a soldier the same as the rest. It doesn't matter what sex I am. I'm here to do a job and that's what I'll do."

They stared at each other, exchanging a wealth of information and emotions without speaking a word—determination, defiance, irritation. *Desire*.

"Hell." Louie dragged a hand through his dark curls, a clear indication of his inner turmoil.

Mac remained glued to the spot, adrenaline pumping hard and fast through her body. She swallowed and mentally shook herself free of the spell she'd fallen under. Louie's presence wouldn't be a problem. She wouldn't let it.

"My accommodation?" she prompted.

"We're full. You'll be sharing with me."

Disbelief held her still. Oh yeah. That would be right. Fate would make her room with temptation on two legs. Not that she'd ever admit her problem to him. She arched her brows, pretending merely idle curiosity. "You?"

"Yeah." He eased away from her and folded his arms across his broad chest, the move drawing her unwilling attention. His sensual mouth kicked up into a mocking smile. "Worried about not being able to keep your hands off?"

Mac snorted. "You wish."

His brown eyes gleamed with the same mischief he'd demonstrated during their time in Fiji. "Grab your gear, Joanna. I'll show you the way." He strode to the door without waiting for her reply.

"The name is Mac." Tight-lipped, she scooped up her bags and stomped after the man, murder on her mind. Work and play. Two very distinct and different things in her life. Joanna played while Mac worked and concentrated on keeping them both alive. Together they made one balanced soldier.

"Our room," Louie said, making the situation sound way more personal than warranted. He pushed the door open and stood aside for her to enter.

Plain and small. A set of bunks lined one wall while the

12

other bore a set of lockers, the top of which doubled as a shelf. A couple of travel magazines and an old newspaper were visible. A wooden desk sat against the third wall of the room, a thin thriller paperback under one leg bringing sturdiness and balance. A slim black laptop took up most of the surface.

"The showers are down the hall. You have the top bunk." He paused, his eyes glinting with a private joke. "You like being on top so that shouldn't be a problem."

Mac gritted her teeth but didn't comment, instead silently giving thanks she wasn't the blushing type.

"We're going out this afternoon for reconnaissance. You'll be riding along."

Mac nodded, always glad to get into the local routine. A regular schedule helped her settle quicker, kept nerves under better control.

"The mess is open at midday for an hour."

"Thanks." Mac dumped her bags and started to unpack. Not a big chore since, like all the others, she traveled light. She sensed rather than heard Louie leave and let a slow, shuddery breath ease free.

A nightmare.

The man had preyed on her mind more than she cared to admit. They'd had some good times in Fiji. Very good. Working with him would be difficult although not impossible. She could cope. Rooming with the man though, that was going to be a problem. The room smelled of him, tempting and seductive. She already knew how it felt when his hands caressed her naked body. Each drift of his fingers, the pads slightly callused and bringing seductive friction with each touch. His confidence.

Oh yeah. He knew his way around a woman's body. Heat collected, pooling low in her belly, bringing an edgy awareness. Uneasiness.

"Damn." She was in trouble here and wise enough to admit it.

Louie Lithgow knew he was in trouble when his first thought was to haul Joanna into his arms, drag her off to his quarters and fuck her.

No, not Joanna. *Mac.*

Although if she thought a masculine-sounding nickname would make everyone ignore her femininity she'd better rethink her strategy. Didn't work, not with the way those khaki pants of hers clung to her arse. The baggy shirt did a better job of disguising her breasts, but since he'd seen her naked, his imagination was quite capable of filling in the blanks.

Cursing under his breath, he headed for the rec room to grab a coffee. Most of the team was there, hanging and attempting to relax until this afternoon's recon. A few of the new arrivals chatted with others more experienced in personal security in Iraq. Louie knew each of the new arrivals were skilled soldiers, used to military ways. They were more relaxed here, but they still counted on each other while out on recon or an actual security detail. He didn't know how Joanna would fit in. The recruitment team should have told him they were expecting a female.

Louie poured himself a black coffee, doctored it with two spoons of sugar and sauntered over to sit with Simon, his second-in-command and closest friend here.

Simon lifted a brow. "Heard there's a woman amongst the new arrivals."

"Yeah."

"What's she look like? What the fuck is she doing in this hellhole?" His clipped English vowels held disbelief.

Louie shrugged, pretended disinterest, and took a slurp of his coffee. "Maybe she's an adrenaline junkie here to make big money like the rest of us."

He'd thought about her often, even more than he'd thought about home and his friends Nikolai and Jake. Now she was here and fighting the same dirty war as him. A picture formed before he could censor it. Blood.

The acrid scent of cordite. Shouts. Masculine curses. A feminine scream— Louie shuddered, his flesh prickling into goose bumps at the all-too-real scenario. *Damn.* He ignored the racing of his heart and took another sip of coffee even though it tasted like mud.

Simon nodded. "Who's she rooming with?"

"Me." Louie set his coffee cup on the low wooden table in front of them and glared at his mate, daring him to comment.

Simon pursed his lips in a soundless whistle, eyes lighting with amusement. "So that's the way of it."

"It's not what you think." *Dammit, he didn't want to sound defensive.* "I want to keep an eye on things. We're here to do a job and I want to make sure nothing gets in the way of that." Louie cursed inwardly, struggling for control because he wanted to smack the smirk off his mate's face.

"As long as she can do the job."

"She has both experience and qualifications otherwise they wouldn't have given her the job. We'll know how she handles herself soon enough." Louie hated the idea of Joanna seeing action, didn't want to imagine a bullet piercing her beautiful skin or a car bomb blowing her away or one of the hundred other ways a person could die over here.

Snarling under his breath, he grabbed his coffee.

Somehow he was going to have to slot Joanna into the position of soldier instead of seeing her as a woman. Kind of difficult when all he could think of was the snug warmth of her pussy and how it felt while clutching his cock.

Parting from her at the airport in Nandi had been one of the most difficult things he'd ever done. He thought about his vibrant, beautiful lover often, a bright light on his horizon when the tension of constant war got to him. He'd made himself a promise during one particularly bad day when they'd lost a man. During his next furlough, he'd intended to find Joanna, to pick up right where they'd left off. Either that or face madness because she'd taken up residence in his head. He hadn't been able to stop thinking about her.

Instead she'd found him.

Sorta fucked up his plans, added a few spanners and generally made the situation messy. He was her boss. He couldn't make a move on her without it looking as if he was using his position. Sexual harassment. Hell, even if she were willing, it wouldn't look good to the other men.

Conversation stopped dead and Louie glanced up to see Joanna—Mac—pausing in the doorway. He watched her closely, as did every other male in the room. Louie caught the slight tightening of her jaw, the firming of her mouth, but only because he knew her intimately. Her breasts rose in a quick breath, and she glided to the coffee machine and the two men standing beside it.

"This oughta be interesting," Simon muttered.

Louie wanted to leap to his feet, shove the other men out of the way and stake his claim. His hand gripped the mug of coffee, the color leaching from his knuckles. Going against every instinct screaming through him, he calmly took a sip, watching the interaction in the same way as the other men. Slowly the tension eased from his shoulders. Although he couldn't hear the conversation, it was obvious Mac wasn't falling for the flirtatious lines from Charlie or Garrett, one of their medics.

"Probably a first for those two," Simon spoke Louie's thoughts aloud.

"Do them good," Louie said.

Simon studied her intently. "Nothing out of the ordinary."

"Your wife will be pleased to hear it." Louie took care to keep his voice neutral. No way was he giving his mate an opportunity to rib him. Besides, Simon hadn't seen her as he had with her hair spilling down her naked back, her lips wrapped around a cock. His cock...

Bloody hell. He had to stop his thoughts tripping into sexual territory. He studied Mac, trying to see what Simon saw. A tall woman dressed in khaki trousers, a sand-colored shirt, which didn't exactly flatter or showcase her curves, and sturdy boots. He couldn't fault her for that. This was work and her attire was suitable for the job and climate. She didn't look much different from any of the others, which meant she wouldn't present a special target for the militia forces. From a distance they wouldn't realize she was a woman. Also a good idea in this Muslim country. She wore her brown hair tied back, confined in a low knot of some sort. Because it was bound so tightly, none of the rich array of colors reflected in the light, the strands of red and gold. In the sun her unbound hair had reminded him of autumn leaves. Her skin carried a light tan and up close there was a smattering of freckles across the bridge of her pert nose, just as he remembered. Thick, lush lashes surrounded golden-brown eyes—whiskey eyes he'd called them in Fiji—while her mouth was curved and luscious, the bottom lip plumper than the top.

Mac might look the soldier now, but Louie would bet if any of them saw her the way he'd first seen her, dressed in a golden bit of nothing, swaying on the dance floor, they might reevaluate their opinions. He certainly wasn't fool enough to let them into the secret.

Mealtime came and went. Louie listened to the questions and conversations and learned at the same time as the other men. Bosnia, Papua and New Guinea and

Afghanistan. Mac had seen plenty of action in hot spots around the world.

Time for the route reconnaissance in preparation for the CBS jaunt the next day. Louie stood and several others did as well, including Mac. He liked to throw the new recruits into the action straightaway, and they had another reconnaissance group going out tomorrow. The trick to successful protection lay in careful planning, checking and rechecking planned routes for potential problems.

Outside, two of their specially armored cars waited for them along with local drivers who spoke the language. His men donned protective vests and hats and readied weapons, both rifles and pistols, before climbing into the vehicles. The new recruits waited for instruction.

"You two in the back vehicle. Follow Simon's instructions. He'll explain about the things to look for. Mac, Tai, you're with me in the lead vehicle."

Mac entered the rear of the vehicle with Tai and Garrett while Louie took the passenger seat. He checked the link between the cars. "Come in, Simon."

"Louie, we're good to go." Simon's voice crackled through the radio.

"Basically we're checking the route we'd like to use to take the CBS reporters tomorrow afternoon. If it's a no-go, we'll try the longer alternative route. Anything that raises your suspicion let me know, particularly if you see anyone watching us and talking on their mobile or using it to take photos." Louie rattled through the rest of his spiel automatically. The hair at the back of his neck prickled insistently, a sensation he knew not to ignore.

He scanned their surroundings as the driver pulled out of the compound. Nothing out of the ordinary. Locals going about their business, mostly males, with a few women dressed in head-to-foot black, their faces covered while they scurried down the edges of the road, carrying shopping baskets. Two battered vehicles drove slowly past, a radio blaring in one.

The palm trees they passed provided little respite from the hot afternoon sun. Sweat trickled down Louie's back, making his shirt cling, his skin itch. He ignored the discomfort to concentrate on their surroundings.

"Man at three o'clock," Mac said in a calm voice.

Louie's gaze swiveled to the location she indicated. He spotted the man seconds before the ruins of a bombed building hid him from view.

"He's moving off," Mac said.

"Checkpoint," the driver muttered, slowing the vehicle.

Louie cursed and slipped his gun out of sight but retained it in his hand. Local soldiers ran the roving checkpoints. They shot first and asked questions later.

Cooperation and patience were key to remaining alive. If all else failed the driver would barrel straight through and hope for the best.

"Tell him we're going east," Louie instructed the driver.

The driver spoke rapidly in the local dialect, answering questions fired at him by the young soldier.

Louie relaxed fractionally when the soldier waved them through. "Good man," he said to the driver.

They made excellent progress despite the slow-moving traffic and the wait for a British army convoy to pass through an intersection. Overhead, a Black Hawk helicopter buzzed like a whining mosquito, drawing sporadic fire from a patch of undergrowth.

"Don't like this," Simon said via the radio. "More gunfire than usual. Not many locals either. What's your gut say?"

"Something's going on," Louie agreed, the back of his neck still prickling in warning. Danger lurked in the shadows. Somewhere. "Guess our quiet period is over. Can you see anything?"

Up ahead, two vehicles jammed on their brakes, coming to an abrupt stop. Behind the second recon car, another stopped, blocking their retreat. Magically, the few remaining locals faded into the background, leaving a deserted street.

"Ambush," Simon shouted.

Gunfire cracked directly behind them. A signal. Bullets rained down. From the front. From the rear. The rat-a-tat-tat of guns filled Louie's ears, made them ring.

"Fire!" Simon hollered through the radio.

Louie concentrated on the two vehicles in front. "Shoot to kill." Simon would watch their six, but he gave orders anyway. "Mac, check our rear."

Like a freak hailstorm, the bullets pelted their vehicle. Cautiously, Louie opened his door. Crouched behind. Fired.

Mac, Tai and Garrett fired with rapid precision from behind lowered windows. The jackhammer of AK-47 assault rifles echoed between the buildings, replaying in his head. All the time he was aware of Mac behind him. Part of him wanted to throw her back in the vehicle, keep her safe. He started to move and froze when a bullet whizzed past his cheek.

"Fuck." He ducked behind the door, forced himself to concentrate. Just him and his weapon in hand. Shoot to kill. Fire. Fire. *Fire!* Bullets struck the door, kicked up dust until his eyes smarted. Men shouted. Somewhere in front of him, a man shrieked for help, his French accent casting him as one of the insurgent volunteers from abroad. Fanatics, they came from all over the world to fight for the cause.

Time slowed, the insurgents returning a barrage of fire. Sweat dripped down Louie's face. He swiped it away, fear clutching at his chest. They couldn't keep this up for much longer. Should they make a run for it? He fired another round of shots, assessing the situation, making decisions.

"Rear car is retreating," Simon reported in a terse voice. *Thank you, God. Something was going right.*

The driver moved the second car up, giving them better cover. Another of the insurgents fell to the ground, didn't move. Grimly, Louie fired until all return fire ceased. The guns of his men fell silent, but they remained watchful. Louie cautiously peered around the door to scan the vicinity. When no one moved, he ordered everyone back into the vehicles.

They'd been bloody lucky this time. He swiped a weary hand over his face. Mac... Damn! Thoughts of her had distracted him. Time to get a grip. He'd get them all killed if he didn't start thinking with his head instead of his dick.

"We'll keep going," he said into the radio, still rattled by his uncharacteristic veer from commander to man. Their driver pulled away. They passed several bodies, the dark patches of blood a stark contrast to the dusty ground.

"What happened to the plastic surgeon who stood too close to the fire?" Garrett asked, breaking the tense silence.

"No idea," Louie said.

"He melted," Garrett said with a trace of smugness.

There was a moment's startled silence and then the driver started laughing. Louie found himself smirking.

"Jeez, Garrett," Mac said with a groan.

"Garrett telling his lame jokes again?" Simon asked, his voice crackling through the radio.

"Yup," Louie replied. "You really don't want to know."

"I've got one," Simon said, continuing before anyone could protest. "Why are four-legged animals bad dancers?" He paused then said, "Because they have two left feet."

Louie snorted. "That was worse than Garrett's." But it had done the job and broke some of the lingering tension.

They recommenced their drive to the site of the bombing the CBS reporters wanted to film. Louie didn't relax. Neither did his men. They continued their scrutiny of the men, women and children and scanned other vehicles. Up ahead, vehicles came to a halt.

Louie narrowed his eyes against the glare. "Hell, not again."

"US Army is here," Simon said tersely.

Louie watched the soldiers scurry around, took in the equipment they carried. "Could be a bomb."

"Should we go back? Try a detour?"

"Might be quicker." Call him antsy, but he didn't like

cooling his heels in a line of traffic. They were stationary targets. Louie turned to the driver. "Can we take an alternative route?"

"We can try," the driver said.

Louie nodded. "It won't hurt to do a reconnaissance of an alternative route." He and Simon discussed tactics. "Let's do it," Louie said finally.

Their driver backed up, retreating in the direction they'd come from. The streets were eerily quiet until a blast rocked their vehicle. The sound followed seconds later, vehicle debris flying through the air. A hunk of metal struck the window on Louie's side of the vehicle. He flinched, cursing as the reinforced glass cracked under the impact. Luckily it held. *A bloody bomb.*

Simon's voice crackled through the radio. "Everyone okay?"

"Yeah. You?"

"No need to visit the shithouse in a hurry," Simon said.

Behind him, Mac, Tai and Garrett chuckled, and Louie felt the grin stretch his lips. "Thanks for sharing," he said dryly.

Their driver proceeded cautiously down the road, dodging a pothole and driving around a burned-out vehicle waiting for removal. Its tires were flat, the spots of olive paint on the rear telling him it was an army vehicle.

"Go slow," he cautioned. "Looks like this vehicle was attacked recently."

"Vehicle wasn't there yesterday," Simon said.

"Copy that." Which meant they could face problems along this road.

Their driver slowed. "Dead-end," he said, indicating the building that had come under fire from a bomb strike, the debris blocking the road.

"Did you see that?" Garrett demanded. "Nine o'clock. The sun glinted off something."

They all stared intently at the area the medic indicated. Tension radiated within the vehicle.

"There. I saw it again," Garrett said. "It's another ambush."

"Back up." Louie had barely spoken when an RPG fired, gouging a hole where their vehicle had stood mere seconds before. "Get us out of here."

Another shot fired, the rocket-propelled grenade rocking their vehicle before they turned the corner onto another street.

"Is it always like this?" Mac asked in a faint voice.

Garrett laughed. "This is more action than we've seen in the last month."

"Right." Mac didn't sound as if she believed him.

"It's true," Louie said. "It's always like this. Periods of

quiet followed by frantic activity."

The driver tried another route, and although someone fired at them and they had to wait at another checkpoint for over an hour, they managed to get to the building CBS wanted to visit and work out a safe route for the trip the following day.

They arrived back at base with a sense of relief.

"Good job, men." It took Louie an instant to realize he'd lumped Joanna in with the rest of the men. She'd done her job calmly. Professionally. This might work after all. Yeah, as long as he pictured her in dusty khaki for the next six months.

Mac climbed out of the vehicle both jazzed and jittery after the long recon. It was always the same for her—she needed to wind down after seeing action. Some chose alcohol, available in Iraq if a person had contacts. She preferred a clear head and physical exercise. Usually she'd go for a run. Not an option here, although she'd heard they had a gym with weights. That would do.

"Are we free now?" she asked.

"Yeah, unless we have something else come up," Louie said. "Great job today."

"Thanks." Mac hurried through the mess, heading for her room. Once inside, she double-checked the safety on her weapon and set it aside. The bedroom door opened and closed while she was shrugging out of her protective vest.

"You okay?" Louie asked, placing his gun on top of the lockers.

"Yeah."

He studied her closely, an enigmatic expression in place. "Yeah?"

Mac tried to cover her jitters. Didn't happen. A huge shudder gave her away. Her groan of dismay squeezed past tight lips. Breathless, she sucked in a lungful of air and immediately wished she hadn't. Louie. His large presence filled the room. The urge to jump him brought another shudder. "Gotta go to the gym," she muttered, glancing away to grab a T-shirt.

"Joanna."

Her head jerked up. Hell, she hadn't heard him move, didn't realize he was so close. Her skin crawled, but it was different this time. Arousal colored her body's reaction, and she knew she was hip deep in trouble. She sucked in a deep breath, struggling for equilibrium. Louie's scent hit her first, along with a hint of gun and dust, the tang of sweat.

"I can give you what you need." His dark whisper blasted warm, moist air over her cheek. *Sweet, sweet temptation.*

"We shouldn't." She understood exactly what he meant.

29

Pictured it clearly. Her body hummed with approval. *God, she was so weak.* "We won't." *Yeah, that was better.*

"No one needs to know apart from us." His husky voice held temptation.

She trembled, her nipples so tight with need they ached. She wanted him so bad. No, not him. The physical act of sex. That's what she wanted.

"Do you think you're the only one who needs to burn off adrenaline? We can help each other."

"You scratch my back, I scratch yours?" And what would happen if he blabbed to everyone here at their base?

"Basically." He cupped her cheek, and she noticed the fine tremor of his hand. The sight reassured her, told her this wasn't just a line and a means to get his rocks off. He needed the same release, the same basic physical activity to rid his body of stress.

Mac relaxed against his hard chest, quivering with tension of a different sort now. She couldn't do this, could she?

But it had been so long. She'd slept with one man since her holiday in Fiji—a one-night stand that had left her feeling empty and dirty. She slid a furtive glance at Louie. Another crime to throw at his feet. He'd spoiled her for other men, not that she'd ever admit it. That would give him ideas when she had no intention of anything more than casual. As long as neither of them gossiped to others, it might work. Hell, she was really considering agreeing to his proposition.

"Are you up for this?"

Mac swallowed at Louie's husky words, glanced at the bulge in his trousers. He was. Concealing a smirk, she lifted her head to meet his direct gaze with one of her own. He wanted her to agree verbally, so there would be no misunderstanding later. Fair enough. No problem.

"This is our secret? None of the others will know?"

"Not from me." His steady demeanor and the sincerity in his brown eyes convinced her he spoke the truth. She could trust him.

She nodded, reassured by what she knew of him from personal experience. "Okay. No strings or promises. Just sex." Mac held her breath, waited for his reply.

Just sex. Yeah, she could do that. Shove it in the casual slot and pretend that's where it went. Mac thought about David and scowled. She didn't do romances with military men these days. *Never.* Sex, but not love and romance.

"I agree. Can we start now?" Despite his military experience and his seniority, the naughty-boy twinkle in his eyes made her want to laugh. He'd made her laugh in Fiji. They'd had so much fun, swimming, snorkeling, walking hand in hand on the white sandy beach. And the nights. They'd danced, dined, and made love. Mac sighed, her body tingling from the memories.

"Yeah," she said, striving for honesty and ignoring the little voice in her head telling her this wasn't a good idea. "I need to work off the buzz."

"That we can do," he said, reaching for her. His strong arms and familiar scent surrounded her. She felt the steady throb of his heart, smelled the dusty cotton of his shirt, and relaxed against his hard chest, slipping into the comfort he offered.

"You ready to fuck?" he whispered against her ear. The blunt words sent a dark thrill sizzling through her veins.

Mac tipped back her head. "Bring it on." She unbuttoned his shirt with deft fingers, the fiery-hot flesh beneath sending an urgent message to her brain. *Hers.*

Before she could touch, he kissed her. Hard. Urgent. Full of need and tinged with desperation. Blood roared through her veins. She tunneled her hands into his hair and fought for sensual control. Nothing gentle. All rough demand. They nipped, ate at each other's lips. Warm, sleek tongues stroked and danced while urgent hands explored.

Skin. She needed skin.

Mac ran her hands over tanned pectorals, dug in her fingernails, reveled in his hiss. Roughly, she yanked his belt to gain access to the rest of his luscious body. Mac ripped open the fly of his trousers, tearing at the zipper.

"God, let me," he said. "Don't want an unexplained injury."

Mac laughed and stepped back to shuck her clothes. Louie did the same and she stared in unabashed curiosity. Her memory hadn't done the man justice. Not an ounce of extra fat, he was all lean muscle. Sexy ink on his biceps and shoulder. Enticing.

"Now," she said in a hard voice.

"You're not ready."

"Now," she insisted. "I need you now."

Louie scooped her up and dropped her on his narrow bunk. It smelled of him with the faint tang of soap. She didn't have much time to take in anything else. He covered her, taking a nipple in his mouth. One of his hands parted her legs, stroked along her slit. He grunted.

"You on the Pill?"

"Yeah."

"I've been over here since Fiji."

In other words, he hadn't slept with anyone since her. In Fiji they'd used condoms.

"You don't need a condom."

"Good." The word hissed from between his lips as he pushed into her tight pussy.

Mac groaned and he stilled. She didn't want talk.

Action. That's what she needed. Mac arched up, impaling herself fully. Good. *So good.*

Louie pulled back and started thrusting in deep, even strokes. In. Out. Mac trembled, loving the hard feel of his body, the maleness of him, and his scent. God, she'd dreamed about his scent for months. It was something unique to him with just a hint of lemon and spice. She gripped his shoulders, digging in her fingernails, silently urging him on. Harder. Faster.

His mouth latched on to a nipple while his blunt fingers roughly stroked her other breast. The nip of pain hurtled her toward climax. She clenched her inner muscles, clamping down on his cock. Louie groaned, stroked her again. Once. Twice. A third time and she flew apart, clit and channel jumping with spasms of acute pleasure.

She was vaguely aware of Louie coming. He stilled, his lungs working like bellows. Louie rolled, taking her with him until they both lay on their sides. He pushed her head against his chest, cuddling while they drifted down from the high. Not exactly the way *just sex* went, but Mac went with the flow, savoring the warmth and the closeness of another body.

Mac had good friends in the military and kept in contact with them. All of them were still in active service. Ties forged under fire were strong but completely different from what Louie made her feel. Cuddling was dangerous, more treacherous than facing insurgents. She knew it, accepted it but still didn't move. Her eyes drifted shut. Just a little longer...

CHAPTER TWO

LOUIE LISTENED TO THE whistling breaths of the woman in his arms and knew he was toast. He'd wondered if his memories were faulty, if he'd built Joanna up into a goddess. Then he recalled her calmness out on recon, her steady participation and snorted inwardly. The woman was a warrior.

His warrior.

She might fight it, but she was his. He'd prove it to her, given time, but knew it wouldn't be easy to muscle past her defenses. First, they both had to stay alive. His heart twisted, acknowledging the flutter of fear for her safety. Instinctively he knew the worst thing he could do was treat her like a woman and try to protect her. Take the safe road. *Fuck, that would make the game dangerous.* He couldn't allow himself to think of anything apart from the job. Stay focused. Soldiers who allowed their concentration to wander died. And suddenly he wanted to live very badly.

Louie stroked his fingers down Joanna's warm, naked back and wondered what would drive a woman to seek out big money in the private sector. With him it was the only way to forge a future. The army and now private security was all he knew. He thought he might buy a small hotel, somewhere warm where the pace moved leisurely. Laid back and easy. But what did Joanna want? Her needs would dictate their future too.

"Mac. Mac." He shook her awake before easing from their embrace. He missed her warmth immediately and fought her allure. Softly, softly.

She blinked at him, her large, startled eyes reminding him of an owl. "Did I fall asleep?"

"Yeah." Louie stood and started dressing, going against every instinct screeching through his mind. "You want to hit the gym?"

A faint frown creased her brow. "The gym?"

"Yeah. Most of the others will be there." He let the words sink in while he grabbed a pair of shorts and a T-shirt.

Joanna. Mac—he had to think of her as Mac—sat up, her mouth cracking open in a yawn. "The gym. Okay."

Louie turned away to grab a pair of socks but not

before a vision of her long, lean body and rounded breasts with pert nipples seared to his retinas. God, he wanted to sink into her pussy again, love her slow and show her tenderness. But he resisted, instead choosing a strategic battle. Instinct told him that was the only way to win the war.

Faint rustling indicated Mac was moving. The woman was staring at his arse. He could practically feel the heat from her eyes. Dammit, she needed to get with the program. How could he keep his hands off if she openly showed her interest?

Louie concentrated on controlling his unruly cock, thinking of cold things while he reached for his shoes.

"You said everyone would be there."

"Yeah, to burn off energy." He could have commented further but didn't want her to get the idea he hadn't liked the way they'd rid themselves of adrenaline.

"Right." The word came out so crisp it damn near saluted.

Louie glanced at her, wary now and a little worried. "The gym is down the hall, third door on the right. You'll probably hear everyone before you get there. Some of the boys like to play basketball." He didn't give her a chance to reply, instead leaving the room, closing the door behind him.

Damn, this relationship stuff was worse than picking his way through a minefield. But worth it. A slow grin bloomed as he remembered her, all liquid fire and warm silk in his arms. Worth the trouble. Still grinning, he strode down the hall. The way he felt right now, he could take on Simon at a little one-on-one basketball and give him a real hiding.

A MISTAKE. WHEN SHE made them, they were doozies. She shouldn't have jumped Louie like that, shouldn't have given in to temptation.

But she had. Done deal.

Mac opened her bag and pulled out a pair of shorts. After a brisk cleanup using her precious store of wet-wipes, she yanked open a locker, saw it was empty and decided to take a moment to unpack. Her body felt well-used, a little sore, but power pulsed through her like the kick of one of those energy drinks. All due to Louie.

The thought brought a frown. She grabbed a sports bra and thrust her arms into it, pulling a gray tank over the top. Five minutes later, she admitted prevarication had become her middle name. Mac jerked open the bedroom door and headed for the gym. If Louie had told everyone he'd banged her, she'd soon know. The gossip and hits from the other men would make life unpleasant but not impossible. She'd lived through worse.

Rowdy shouts and thumps guided her, as Louie had promised. A faint tang of sweat filled the air along with colorful curses when she walked through the door. The sounds and sights were comforting and familiar, part of the male-dominated world she inhabited.

Most of the men were playing a boisterous game of basketball and paid her no attention. So much for her ego. And maybe she was guilty of judging Louie by her ex-fiancé David. He'd liked to brag about his sex life, something she'd discovered late in the piece. It was one of the things they'd argued about before he'd told her to forget their engagement and sauntered away without looking back. A bitter snort escaped. The perfect relationship was a fallacy perpetrated by wedding planners.

Mac walked over to the equipment area and worked through a series of stretches to warm her muscles. She glimpsed Louie in the middle of the melee, a symphony of muscles and smooth moves as he ducked and dribbled the ball down the makeshift court. Mac's body heated instantly. She cursed and started working through the exercise circuit someone had set up. From the start, she pushed herself, trying to outrun her wanton thoughts.

Lift. Pump. Grunt. Her breathing deepened, heart thudding with the exercise. The man might be good at releasing the buzz but that didn't mean she needed him. It wouldn't happen again. Yep, she'd keep her hands off, do the job, collect her money and go home to check on her father before grabbing another contract.

Mac moved to the next station still thinking of her father. She needed to check out the email situation. She'd promised to send a note to the head nurse at the home, let her know she'd arrived and how to reach her in case of an emergency. Maybe she should think about getting another cell phone. Nah, the way she killed them off it was becoming expensive. Her lip quivered a fraction when she recalled fishing the last one out of the toilet. It had never worked after that.

Mac grunted, lifting weights that tested her strength. The burn felt good until her arms started shaking on the sixth rep.

"You should have someone spotting you." Simon, Louie's second-in-charge, took the weight from her and set it back on the rack.

Louie stood beside Simon, a frown on his sexy face. Her heart squeezed out three hard, fast beats before she regained control of her breathing.

"You're right," she said, sitting up. Using the bottom

of her tank top, she blotted the sweat off her face. "No excuses, except I needed to push myself."

"Don't do it again," Simon said.

"I won't." She wasn't only talking about the weights, and she saw from Louie's face he guessed the direction of her thoughts.

"We're all going to watch a movie after we clean up. You're welcome since you're part of the team," Louie said.

Probably something with naked women. Mac knew better than to watch a movie with the guys without checking first. This time she'd give it a miss completely. "Thanks, but I need to check my email. Is there somewhere I can do that?"

"Most of the guys have their own laptops," Simon said.

"You can use mine," Louie said. "If you're finished here, I'll log you in."

"Thanks." She stood, feeling uncomfortable with the silence that fell. Rooming together had suddenly become too intimate. Not that she could do anything about it. This was work, the best way to earn lots of money fast and ensure her father had the best healthcare possible.

The three of them headed for their rooms, Simon entering one several doors away from theirs. Mac opened their door and stepped inside. The sharp clunk of the door closing made her jump, even though she was expecting it.

"You okay?"

Mac forced a laugh. "I'm fine. Where are the showers?"

"You passed them on the way to the gym."

Shoot. She hadn't noticed since one man dominated her thoughts. Not good, especially for a soldier.

Louie frowned. "We're not set up for women here. The showers, I mean. There are no cubicles, just showerheads along one wall. Everyone showers together."

"Don't worry. I'm used to sharing. It won't be a problem unless someone grabs something they shouldn't."

His face cleared and she watched a twinkle appear in his eyes. Her stomach lurched in a zap of attraction. "Do I need to warn the men about you? Are you likely to grab?"

Mac spluttered a couple of times before realizing he was kidding. She drew in a sharp breath, strove for control. "I'll try to control myself."

"You're welcome to grab me anytime you want."

Dangerous territory. *Again*. Suddenly the silence between them throbbed with possibilities. "I don't think we should do that again. All I want is to get through my contract alive."

Louie's inscrutable face didn't reveal a thing. "That's what we all want. My laptop is on the desk. Just help yourself whenever you want to use it. The password is Fiji Islands. One word, both with capitals." He grabbed a towel and a navy blue toilet bag and exited their room, leaving her gaping after him.

Fiji Islands.

Mac closed her eyes, struggling to deal with the memories, the emotions he'd tugged to the surface by uttering his password. Unfortunately shutting down her sight made her other senses jump to the fore. Louie's scent wound through her, seductive and enticing. The sexual throb she'd worked off in the gym came back to haunt her big-time. Damn the man.

She grabbed her towel and wiped her face. Although a shower sounded tempting, she decided to wait until the men started their movie before venturing into that territory. They needed to get used to having her around, start thinking of her as one of the boys first.

Mac yanked out the spindly chrome and wood chair and gingerly settled her weight. When nothing disastrous occurred, she settled back and opened the lid of the laptop. It whirred while it powered up and finally she entered the password, *FijiIslands*. Why had the man used those particular words? Her mind sped through the possibilities and kept coming back to the same one. Fiji had meant something to him. But that didn't make sense. Why hadn't he bothered to contact her?

Oh yeah. He wouldn't have been able to because she'd

given him a false name. In the past she'd always been big on keeping her private life separated from her sex life. Her choice of occupation attracted nosy questions, sometimes outright hostility. And she'd found out the hard way not many men liked to share the responsibility for a father who suffered from Alzheimer's. That had been something else she and David had shouted about the night they broke up. Her eyes misted as thoughts of her previously robust father flooded her mind. Ex-army, he'd always seemed larger than life. Seeing him robbed of dignity made her heart ache. Sometimes the loss of pride was worse than the fact he didn't remember her, even on his good days.

Trembling fingers logged in to her email account and her heart beat frantically until she saw she'd only received mail from army friends. No news from the home meant nothing had changed with her father. Her breath eased out with a relieved hiss. Her father had been both pleased and concerned when she'd joined the army. He'd explained the pros and cons of the lifestyle, the danger and positives of the good mates made for life. She'd write him a letter soon. He liked the nurses to read him letters, even though he didn't know who they were from. Strangely, he remembered some of his army life and this familiarity with some of the contents of her letter gave him pleasure.

The door opened without warning and Louie stepped

inside. She gave a girlie gasp and wanted to kick herself. *For God's sake, woman. Grow a set of balls. You have to stop reacting like a startled recruit around him.*

"Everything okay?"

"It's fine. I'm fine." The edge on her words was sharp enough to carve stone. A giveaway of her turmoil. She concentrated on slow, even breaths, unwilling to admit how close she was to the ledge. Seeing Louie had thrown her because she'd thought of him often and her memories had held regret. Add that to her continued grief over her father's decline and yeah, she was off her game. "Put on a shirt."

A smirk bloomed, lighting up his eyes. Man, she was a sucker for a fine pair of eyes. Add a sexy bod and those tattoos to the equation and danger loomed in her future. He prowled closer, his chest as bronzed as it had been in Fiji. Mac studied the white towel, tucked in at his waist, and wondered what it would take to make it fall. Earlier hadn't been about looking, touching—it had been more about mutual craziness. She'd wanted to feel.

"Do I have to remind you about misconduct?"

"It's only misconduct if it's not mutual," Mac muttered. Hell! Had she just said that? She risked a glance, found him grinning and pouted. "I didn't say that. It was a djinn, an evil spirit intent on trouble."

"Look, I know you're worried we've made a mistake. But I want you, Mac. Can't we let it happen and not worry about complications?" He held up his hands when she would've protested. "No, let me say my piece. I like you, but we're here to do a job. The job comes first. Always, because that's the only way any of us leave on our own feet. We can do casual without it blowing up in our faces."

"Use each other," she inserted once again with bite because his words weren't what she wanted to hear, no matter what she told herself.

"Blunt, but basically what I had in mind. Mac, you know me. Better the devil you know."

"True. Yeah, okay." There was something wrong with her, leaving herself open for hurt this way. But damn, it would be wonderful having someone to hold her in the dark of the night when nightmares of death, hers or her father's, stalked her mind. For a few seconds she worried about gossip until she concluded there would be rumors anyway. It was up to her to divert them and show the rest of the men she was the same as them—a soldier doing a job.

Fascinated, Louie catalogued the play of emotions on her face. In Fiji he'd found it difficult to read her. Now she looked vulnerable. A glance at the laptop confirmed she'd checked her private mail. Bad news from home? He didn't know much about her private life. They'd talked books, movies, about her work. Her fictional job. Man, she'd sucked him right in with her cover story about her secretarial job. It made him consider how often she'd used the same story with other men. He hated the thought. Seemed he had a possessive streak when it came to Mac. *Play it cool.* He'd need to use his sniper training, exert the patience he'd learned in the army while waiting for a target.

"I was the last out of the showers, if you want to head that way." The need for personal info, some small snippet simmered through him. "My brother is the lawyer. Apart from that, most of what I told you is the truth."

She nodded. "Thanks for letting me use your laptop. I'm gonna hit the showers."

"Sure." Fuck, she was treating him like a stranger. Louie prowled to his locker, grabbed out a clean shirt and trousers, a pair of boxers and dropped the towel without thinking.

He heard the small whoosh of air from her lungs. When he risked a glance in her direction, she was closing down his laptop. Interesting. He dressed silently, deep in thought. A good soldier always had a plan and a backup one when everything went to crap. "Dinner is at seven," he said.

"Thanks."

Despite wanting to stay, he left the room. His new

mission would be a tough one, but like any hard-fought battle, the victory would taste sweet.

CHAPTER THREE

LOUIE JERKED AWAKE, HEART pounding in the darkness of his room. For an instant he wasn't sure what had woken him then he heard the whimper. *Mac.* Silently, he climbed from the bottom bunk and stood, watching her shadowed face. She appeared young and vulnerable with her hair loose, lying in tangled curls across her pillow. Another sob emerged and her face screwed into a pained grimace.

"Steady, Mac. It's okay." Gingerly he reached out to stroke her arm. Just touching the warm, silky skin gave him all sorts of ideas. He quashed them. When she whimpered for a third time, he scooped her off the top bunk and placed her in his bed. He'd noticed in Fiji how soundly she slept so wasn't surprised when she didn't wake. Although, he'd probably catch hell from her later, this struck him as a good way of chasing away her nightmares. And damn if he wouldn't sleep better with a luscious woman in his arms. Louie slipped into the narrow bunk, pulled her into his arms and sighed with satisfaction when she melted against him. He waited for her to start dreaming again, and when she didn't, he drifted off to sleep with a smile on his face.

Mac woke slowly, toasty warm and content. With the stress of job interviews and setting up her father in the home before she arrived in Iraq, sleep hadn't come easy. It was a surprise to wake up feeling so refreshed.

"Mac? You awake?"

Her head jerked up, connecting with another. Stars danced through her head and tears formed in her eyes. Louie's naked body was plastered against hers and he was pleased to see her. "Ow! What the fuck are you doing in my bed?"

"You're in my bed."

"What? But—"

"You woke me. You were having a bad dream."

Mac wriggled, ceasing only when she realized Louie's cock was becoming happier by the minute. "Why didn't you wake me?"

Louie just looked at her, his dark brows rising while the beginnings of the smile hovered on his sexy lips. "Me and whose army?"

"There was no need to move me," she muttered, silently conceding he had a point.

"I wanted to sleep."

"I— Heck. What time is it?"

"Another hour before we need to move."

"Is that a hint for sex?"

"Nope, but sex is a good idea," he said, his lazy grin pushing against the restraint and good sense she tried to summon. "I'm game if you are."

Lucky for him he didn't follow-up his words with a crude thrust of his hips or something similar because then she would have felt justified in jerking her knee upward into his groin. Subdue a little of that happy morning feeling.

Oh heck. Who the hell was she trying to kid? She wanted him. And he wasn't shy about showing his interest so she knew it was mutual. Weak, she thought. Really weak. A trace away from needy. At least he hadn't asked what she'd dreamed about. Mac didn't think she was up to explaining the fears that rioted through her mind when her defenses were low.

Perhaps sex was a good distraction.

She reached for him, curling her fingers around his shoulders as she forced away thoughts of morning breath. Their mouths met, her heart pounded. Yeah, she was weak-willed when it came to this man. Louie rolled over and almost fell off the bunk. He laughed, lifting her until she draped over him like a blanket.

"T-shirt off," he ordered.

Mac couldn't see any reason to disobey. She wriggled out her sleep shirt and removed her high-cut panties for good measure. Might as well jump in with both feet.

"Watch where you're putting that knee. Your mouth, now that would be a different story."

Mac snorted a laugh. "That could be arranged."

"Really? I'd like that."

Laughing again, Mac moved down the bed, reminded of the fun and playful times they'd had in Fiji. She grasped his cock and teased him by running a finger down his length, pressing a kiss to his hipbone, and nibbling his inner thigh. His sigh of pleasure brought delight. He'd been such a generous lover, making her enjoy returning the favor. Yeah, they'd had a lot of fun in Fiji.

"Not that I'm not appreciating you touching and teasing but we're on a schedule here, soldier."

A reminder of where they were, the different situation they faced. She bent her head and licked across the head of his cock. His groan brought a smile, her mouth stretching around his shaft while the feel, the taste of him contributed to stirring more memories. Heat rioted through her breasts, streaking down to form a ball of fiery sensation low in her belly. She shivered, floating in a dream world where bombs and guns didn't exist. Her tongue lapped lazily, under and over, pulling shudders and shakes from him. When her tongue pressed into his slit, he groaned, his hips jerking violently.

"Joanna," he whispered, his blunt fingers tunneling through her hair, massaging her nape in silent encouragement.

She took him deeper, pushed a little harder. Teased his swollen sac. Caressed the base of his shaft and swallowed around his sensitive tip. His large body trembled, his deep groan and involuntary thrusts telling her he was close. She licked and laved, paying attention to the sensitive underside.

"Hell." Louie pulled away abruptly, breathing hard. Before she could protest, he grabbed her, parted her legs and pushed roughly inside. She was so wet his cock slid to the hilt in one thrust. "Joanna." Her name was an expression of male satisfaction.

"Yes?"

"Nothing."

Mac wanted to ask questions, but he withdrew and steadily pushed back inside, filling her. She clutched his broad shoulders, arching up into his thrusts while sensations built inside her. He nuzzled her throat, nibbled at the fleshy part where neck and shoulder met. The bite of his teeth pulled a muted cry from her.

He lifted his head, stilling while buried deep. "Too much?"

"More," she whispered. "It feels so good." And it did. No wonder her one-night stand had made her feel so dirty. It had been about sex, but this...this was more. The intense rightness of being with Louie. It frightened Mac, made her feel vulnerable. A knot of panic closed her throat. She couldn't have said anything if she'd wanted to. Instead, she held on to Louie, using him like an anchor in a storm. The pleasure built rapidly, each breath a ragged gasp. A sheen of sweat coated their skins, the scent of sex and arousal heavy on the air.

Louie reached between them, smoothed a finger across her swollen nub. Mac wanted to cry out her delight but bit down on her bottom lip, not wanting anyone to hear. Another stroke of his finger sent sensation streaking from her clit. Her pussy rippled, clenching his cock. He drove inside her again, hard and fast, before stilling abruptly with a hoarse moan of pleasure. His eyes were squeezed shut and his head thrown back, his face a contorted mask of what looked like pain. Mac's heart thumped erratically until he opened his eyes, the blaze of chocolate-brown stealing her breath. They stared at each other until she dragged her attention away, panic beating a rapid tattoo against her ribs. She couldn't care for him. This was sex for mutual benefit, just like any casual relationship.

Mac gulped and retreated, separating their bodies without looking at him. "Guess we'd better get moving."

Louie studied her intently and ran his hand across her upper thigh. The callused drag of his fingers pulled a shiver from her. The temptation to linger hovered in the back of her mind.

"Thanks, Mac." He climbed from the bunk and stretched, the ripple of muscles and flex of tattoos a beautiful view to watch.

Disgusted with her girlie gaping, she turned away, reminding herself she was a soldier. She rapidly cleaned up, sending silent thanks for the impulse that led her to pack wet-wipes. They were doing a training session this morning before taking the CBS crew out in the afternoon. No time for a shower. Mac yanked on a pair of panties and pulled khaki trousers over the top.

"I'll see you at breakfast," Louie said, already dressed.

Mac nodded, not trusting herself to speak. Suddenly she had a lump in her throat and the backs of her eyes ached. She reached for a bra, tense shoulders relaxing after she heard the thud of the door. Mac sank onto the bottom bunk and doubled over to hold her head in her hands. Sleeping with Louie was a mistake.

"Stuff it," she muttered, standing to don her sand-colored shirt. Mac dragged a comb through her hair and pulled it into her usual tight knot. Time to move out and face the day. Time to shove all the crap loitering in her mind right to the back and to take her place on the team. Her father was counting on her.

Mac stalked the narrow corridor, pausing at the doorway of the room where they took meals.

"How's it roomin' with Mac?" one of the men asked.

"The same as sharing with any of you lot," Louie retorted. "Except she smells a lot better."

Ribald laughter greeted Louie's words. Mac had known there would be comments because of her sex. She'd expected—hoped—Louie wouldn't mention their sleeping status to anyone and eased out her breath with relief when he diverted the nosy questions while joking with the rest of the men. Lifting her head, she sailed into the room, stopping by the coffee machine to grab a cup.

"Did Louie's snoring keep you awake?" someone asked.

"Nope. I've trained myself to sleep through anything." Mac grinned and grabbed a tray, loading up her plate with food.

"You could room with me," one of the men said, his

suggestive leer saying a hell of a lot more.

"I'd prefer not to room with a shark," Mac said sweetly.

The other men laughed as she'd meant them to, and she moved down the cafeteria-style line.

"Don't you diet?" Simon asked, moving behind her to grab his breakfast.

"Hell no," Mac said. "I'm a soldier and I like food. Do you diet?"

"Got me," Simon said with a grin. "Merely working out which box to stuff you into."

"Now you know. Soldier box." Mac took a space at one of the tables and was soon in the middle of a spirited conversation about rugby and which team was the best in the world. Since they were an international force, there were lots of opinions.

With eating done, they drove out to the training grounds, keeping a wary eye on everyone and everything on the journey there. A distant pop-pop sounded like guns, the tension immediate inside the vehicle until they realized it was kids letting off fireworks.

Soon they were in full training mode. Louie and Simon barked orders at them, hollering instructions and drilling them on what to do if insurgents attempted to kidnap their clients. They ran through the different scenarios countless times until they all reacted on instinct.

The sun beat down from overhead, making Mac glad she'd grabbed a cap. Dust. It was everywhere and blew into their eyes whenever the fickle breeze crept out of hiding. The protective vests didn't help with the heat problem and her shirt clung to her torso until she felt like a wet dishrag—a dirty one.

"Not fast enough," Louie hollered. "Do it again. Mac, you're lagging. Move it!"

"Yes, sir," she muttered, giving him a figurative salute.

Their team moved back into position, along with Simon, the VIP they were supposed to protect.

"Concentrate, Mac. I don't want a bullet in my butt 'cause you didn't move fast enough to take it in yours," Simon said.

"Yeah, Mac," Tai, one of the other men said. "We'd prefer to pick the bullet out of your arse. I don't want to look at Simon's hairy butt."

"My wife likes my hairy butt."

"Some people have no taste," Tai retorted.

"Ready?" Louie hollered.

"Okay, team," Simon said. "Get me through safely this time, and it will be the last run-through. Screw up and we're gonna work through lunch."

"Go! Go! Go!" Tai barked.

This time they moved with precision, scuttling across

the uneven, sunbaked earth like a single unit.

Mac's breath exited in harsh pants, but she ignored the discomfort to concentrate on the job, covering Simon and moving with the rest of the team. They reached the point of safety and stopped. Mac was pleased to see the others were breathing heavily too. It wasn't just her dealing with exhaustion and the heat.

"Good job," Louie said, striding over to them and looking every bit the soldier. His face was harshly drawn and covered with a fine coating of dust, his brown eyes sharp and piercing.

Mac inhaled sharply at the jolt of sexual awareness that shot down her spine. Her skin prickled, and she almost moaned aloud at the heat coalescing between her legs. Biting down hard on her inner lip, she glanced away to scan the countryside. A moving plume of dust snagged her attention. "A vehicle heading this way. Eight o'clock," she said, adding a directional guide for the others to follow.

Apprehension replaced the easy camaraderie of a job well-done. Simon grabbed a pair of binoculars. "It looks like a friendly."

"Why didn't they call?" Louie barked. "Fall back to the vehicles."

Tension ratcheted up, each soldier moving into a defensive position while they waited for the vehicle to arrive. The driver slowed and two men climbed from the rear.

"What the devil is he doing here?" Simon said.

Louie narrowed his eyes, squinting because of the sun. "No doubt Carolina Eastern sent them. She has him wound around her little finger."

Simon scowled. "Rumor is she's sleeping with him."

"So they say," Louie said with a derisive snort.

Mac didn't recognize the men, but the others relaxed. She took her cue from them.

"Wait here," Louie said. "Cover me."

The fact they needed to take precautions, despite knowing the occupants of the vehicle, reiterated the dangers. Not that Mac needed the reminder. The drive out here, past bombed buildings and discarded vehicles drove home the monsters lurking in the shadows. While the whitewashed villages might appear idyllic, some of the locals were distinctly unfriendly, glaring at them as their convoy drove past. According to Garrett, they'd had rocks chucked at them before.

Worry for Louie surfaced, and Mac squelched it immediately. She didn't have time or the luxury to care for someone else. Despite his Alzheimer's, her father retained his fitness. He needed her. Not even the life insurance she'd arranged would be enough to give him the long-term care he required. No, she had to keep a distance between her and Louie. It was better for both of them. *Safer.*

"I wonder what that's about," Simon said.

"Probably another job," one suggested.

"Maybe." Simon's eyes narrowed at the distinctive sound of a chopper in the distance. "Maybe not."

Louie returned. "Let's get back to base."

Like the others, Mac wondered about the meeting, and what had been so important for someone to make a special trip to see Louie.

During the return trip, they had to drive around the scene of a roadside bomb, the plume of black smoke visible long before they saw the site. American soldiers waved them past, and they arrived back at base without further incident.

"I'm for the showers," Tai said.

Good idea, Mac thought. They were lucky they had plentiful water. In the past she'd soldiered in places where they'd gone days without water and suffered through severe restrictions on use. She would never take running hot-and-cold water for granted again.

Mac headed for her room, deciding to check her email again before hitting the shower. Give the rest time to shower before she ventured in there. She'd scarcely powered up Louie's laptop when he arrived. He pulled out another of the spindly chairs and straddled it to face her, a tense expression on his face.

"What?"

"CBS has heard we have a woman on staff," Louie said. "That's what the men wanted to discuss earlier, and I've just had a follow-up call from Carolina Eastern."

"That's a bad thing?"

"They want to use you as protection while they interview some of the local wives and other women." Louie's tone told her he didn't like the idea.

"I thought protection is our main purpose."

"Yeah, it is. This is different. There would be one female journalist and you with the locals. A team of men can go with you, but they'd need to remain outside for the entire interview."

"But there could be anyone inside the building with the women," Mac said.

"My point exactly. They're gonna talk to the top guys. Probably offer them better money as an enticement to go ahead." His brown gaze pierced her. "I don't like it."

Mac nodded, digesting everything he'd said. "Are your concerns part of the job or private?"

"Both." Louie never hesitated. "You've already proven you're a fine soldier. You have guts and can do the job. You've impressed the rest of the team, and that's no easy feat."

Mac forced herself to look away, to keep her hands clasped in her lap instead of reaching for him. "This thing between us is casual. We can't afford to allow emotions to get into the way." She struggled with the lump lodged in her throat, swallowing to make speech easier. It was straightforward when they were out on the job. She didn't have any problems while she had the job to focus her attention. It was during the downtime when her willpower lagged.

"I know, Joanna. I agree with everything you're saying."

"So, what's the problem?"

"No problem," Louie said, but she could tell he was avoiding the truth. Hell, they both had their heads stuck in the desert sand.

"Are you going to have a shower?"

"Yeah," Louie said.

Mac nodded and picked up her shower gear. "You coming now?" This would be a hell of a test, but one she was determined to ace. If she kept her feelings and emotions corralled inside their room, that would work.

She and Louie walked down the corridor to the showers. There were still quite a few guys showering and in various stages of undress. Mac ignored them. She ignored the small break in the teasing chatter and chucked her gear down on a wooden seat at the far end. Without looking at anyone, she stripped and turned on a shower, washing briskly. The showerhead beside her burst into life and from the corner of her eye, she saw Louie.

After a brief silence, the rest of the guys started to chatter again. Mac soaped the dust and sweat from her body. It would take a couple of weeks before they thought of her as a soldier instead of a female. This time she was glad Louie was here with her. None of the men would try anything with him around. None of them had asked any probing questions about her background yet, only the general stuff, but when they did, she had a cover story ready for them. The only thing was, she'd have to use a different photo when she showed them shots of her fiancé. Somehow, she didn't think it was a wise move to show the photos of her and Louie in Fiji to the rest of the team.

CHAPTER FOUR

AFTER THE INITIAL BLAST of hot water, Louie switched the tap to cold and willed his body not to react to Mac's presence. He grabbed the soap and cleansed his body with rapid efficiency. Switching off the water, he picked up his towel and noticed a couple of the others sneaking a look at Mac. He nailed them with a glare and hoped like hell the expression cried boss man instead of possessive lover. The men looked away with alacrity and a burst of satisfaction filled him. They'd received the message.

He left the shower block with his towel wrapped around his waist. By the time Mac arrived back in the room, draped in an oversized T-shirt, he'd dressed.

"They give you any trouble after I left?" Although he'd appreciated the matter-of-fact way she'd showered, part of him had wanted to grab a towel and hide her from the other men. A problem. Hesitation or worry about another person could foul things up during a protection sortie and cause a casualty or death. He had to get a grip on his emotions.

"No problems," she said, grabbing plain cotton underwear from her locker. "I'm used to staring. They'll forget I'm female after a while." She whipped the T-shirt over her head and started to dress.

He wouldn't forget in a hurry, not after experiencing the silken clutch of her pussy around his cock. Damn, no sane man would forget that. "Good." Louie grabbed the seat in front of his laptop and signed in to check his email. His right hand trembled but he carried on doggedly as he hunted and pecked at the keys.

Louie ignored the slide of fabric and thought of his mate Nikolai and his wife Summer. He'd laughed at Nikolai, given him a hard time and encouraged Summer while she'd driven his friend mad. He hadn't understood his friend's mental pain at the time, why he'd fought to keep his hands off the woman who had jumped feetfirst into his life. He understood now. It was the basic battle of mind and body that produced the stress. He wanted to touch Mac, stake his claim. His hands trembled and his stomach knotted during his inner battle.

Yeah, he knew about conflict.

Mac wasn't interested in a relationship. She'd lied to him in Fiji and given him a false address when they'd parted. And they couldn't have an open relationship here. It would set a bad example to the rest of the men and create morale problems. A six-month contract was long enough without romantic challenges thrown into the mix.

Louie let his breath ease out and he forced himself to concentrate on the tropical scene on the screen. Another property for sale. He clicked on the other views.

"That looks nice. Are you planning a holiday when your contract ends?"

"I'm retiring after this contract."

"Yeah?" Mac pulled up the seat beside him, her face glowing with curiosity. "What are you thinking of doing?"

"Buying a business. A bar or a backpackers' hostel. Something like that." He'd never told anyone except Nikolai and Jake, his best mates, the men he'd gone through Special Air Service training with and fought beside before he'd gone into private security with Chesterton UK to earn some big money.

"Where abouts?" Mac peered over his shoulder, a wave of soap and shampoo filling his senses. She sure smelled better than his previous roommates.

"Somewhere touristy and preferably warm. I don't like

the cold."

Mac chuckled. "Me neither. Winter in Afghanistan was hell, which is why I headed to Fiji for my holiday."

"Why did you give me a false address?" He hadn't meant for the conversation to turn personal, but since it was too late now, he admitted he wanted to know. Hadn't their time together meant anything to her?

"Most guys don't understand about my job. They don't understand how I can spend months in the company of other guys and remain faithful. I've learned it's easier to tell people what they want to hear." Mac stared at the screen while she spoke, obviously unwilling to look at him. "You weren't exactly truthful with me either."

"The address I gave you was real. If you'd contacted me there, I would've replied to you eventually. It's my friend's place."

"Is he army?"

"We were in the SAS together."

Mention of the SAS wrenched her attention off the computer screen. He smiled, and after initial hesitation, she grinned back at him.

"SAS, huh? What made you leave?"

"My mate Nikolai was injured. He's married now and trains the upcoming SAS soldiers. Jake, the other guy we went through training with, is still in active service. I decided I wanted to retire and get a life. Private security offered good money."

Mac nodded. "I hear you."

"You in it for the money too?"

"Yeah."

Louie's brows rose. He'd hoped for a bit more than that. "What are you going to do once your contract is over?"

"Sign up for another one," she said, standing. "I'm going to the mess. You coming?"

"I want to send a couple of emails first."

"See you later." The door opened and closed after her.

Louie cursed. She'd run for cover the moment he mentioned her reasons for working in private security. Most of the guys here wanted quick money. They wanted to buy houses and get a head start in life, pay off debts. Some weren't qualified for anything else. He was tired of fighting, sick of war. In his thirties now, he wanted to buy his own slice of paradise and kick back on the beach. In the past, he'd thought of a woman in the picture. Now she had a face.

Joanna.

He wanted to retire with her at his side. He wanted to amble hand in hand down a pristine beach and watch the sunset. Then he wanted to wander home and make sweet love to his woman, to Joanna.

Louie sent his emails, including one to Nikolai, asking if he knew Mac or someone who'd served with her in the past. Her reticence had fueled his curiosity. Mac was the first person he'd encountered who didn't want to talk.

Louie sent the email and signed off.

When he arrived in the mess, most of the guys were playing poker, Mac included.

Shit, he should have warned her these guys were card sharks. She wouldn't save money that way.

"That's me done," Simon said in disgust. "I'm out."

Mac laughed and raked the pile of chips toward her. "I think I've cleaned everyone out." She raised her brows and glanced in his direction. "Can I talk you into a few hands?"

"Don't take her up on it, Louie. She's a hustler," Simon said.

"Yeah," Tai said. "Where did you learn to play like that?"

"My father." Mac's smile died a fraction before she forced it into a wide beam. Louie didn't think the others noticed. He did. Every little clue added to her mystique.

"Maybe he could give me some tips," Simon said. "I'm not playing with you again. My wife will kill me if I keep losing at poker."

"Bawk. Bawk. Bawk." One of the guys made flapping motions with his arms.

"Fuck off," Simon said good-naturedly at their laughing

71

jeers.

The food arrived. Louie grabbed a plate and thought about the job they needed to do this afternoon. He walked through to the small room he used as an office, taking his lunch with him. He contacted their head office and spoke to his immediate boss about the request from CBS.

"They want Mac to go along as protection with their female journalist when she interviews some of the local women."

"How is she working out?" his boss asked.

"She's a pro. Calm under fire," Louie said. "She fits in well with the rest of the team."

"CBS haven't contacted us yet. Who spoke to you about Mac? Carolina Eastern?"

Louie scowled. "How did you guess? She rang me after we met up with some of her team. That woman is gonna drive me to drink with her demands to take her here and there. We're not running a bloody taxi service. Each jaunt takes hours of planning. You could remind her of that next time you speak to her. And tell her that we put our lives on the line each time we have to research a route through the city."

"She knows the rules. Don't let her push you."

"I don't, but that doesn't stop her trying. I'd better go. We're leaving in half an hour."

"Call in when you're back."

"Sure thing," Louie said, disconnecting the call.

He ate his lunch while his mind dwelled on Mac or rather on Joanna. One woman. Two separate identities. He'd thought about Joanna often since Fiji, even tried to contact her at the false number. He'd shrugged away the disappointment when he'd failed and moved on, or at least that's what he'd thought. The minute he'd seen her again he'd known differently. Sharing a room, holding and making love with her had shown him the truth.

He wasn't over Joanna. Not by a long way.

Louie laughed, the dry sound one of derision because the joke was on him. He wanted Joanna. He wanted to keep her and run the bar he intended to purchase with her at his side. It was equally clear to him that Joanna wasn't open to happy ever after.

Mac had secrets, and Louie had no idea whether there was a man involved or not. He shoved the remains of his lunch away, the sandwich he'd eaten lying like a lump in the pit of his stomach at the thought of another lover.

Hell. Louie raked his hand through his hair and stood to prepare for their afternoon assignment. Things to do. Personal matters had no place on a military mission.

MAC SCANNED THE ROADSIDE, narrowing her eyes against the glare of the sun while she searched for warnings of potential trouble. A market was in full swing on a side street, and she caught a glimpse of a fruit and vegetable stall, the deep purple of aubergine, green of okra and red of tomatoes a splash of color against the dusty road and nondescript buildings. The mission wasn't over until they'd delivered their VIPs back to their quarters. The driver slowed for a checkpoint and they all automatically lowered their weapons, placing them out of sight.

"Tell them we're on our way home," Louie ordered crisply.

Up ahead, gunfire echoed. The local military officer waved them through impatiently while barking orders to his men.

"Hold," Louie snapped when he sensed weapons moving out of hiding. "We don't want any trouble. No photos," he barked at the cameraman in their vehicle. "We'll draw attention. Wait until we know what's going on."

Mac noticed Carolina Eastern's clipped nod at the cameraman. The woman had balls of steel and was calm under fire, but Mac didn't like the way the reporter scrutinized her and had done since they'd first met earlier this afternoon. The hair at the back of her neck prickled, a portent of a bad omen.

The gunfire intensified up ahead, the locals exchanging return fire. Uneasiness ratcheted up inside Mac and sweat tricked down her spine beneath her cotton shirt and heavy protective vest.

"Use the alternative route," Louie said to the driver when a spray of bullets kicked up dust to the right of their vehicle.

Carolina leaned forward between the seats. "I want to report the story."

"No," Louie said immediately.

"I need to report stories as they happen. It's my job." Carolina's crisp diction and New York twang indicated her determination.

"We're paid by your network to keep you safe," Louie countered.

Mac wanted to add her five cents so badly her jaw ached with the tension of keeping her mouth shut. The woman was a pain in the backside. Demanding as hell. None of the team liked her. Dressed well though. Mac really coveted her leather boots. Must have cost a fortune. Mac continued to monitor the area, ducking, and yanking the cameraman by the collar when a shot fired in their direction. A metallic ping told her the shot had hit their vehicle. A second shot glanced off the door. Too damn close.

The driver floored it, tires shrieking as they fought for purchase. The rear of the vehicle swayed before it picked up speed. A cloud of dust obscured vision.

"Everyone okay?" Louie shouted.

"I wanted to film this for a report," Carolina said with clear sarcasm.

Mac and Garrett shared a look.

"We're all good." Mac ignored Carolina's growl of frustration.

Simon radioed, the static worse than usual. "Tai's hit," he said. "Upper arm. We've stemmed the bleeding okay. He'll live."

"I'm complaining to the network," Carolina snarled.

Louie turned to glare at her, eyes flat with anger. "You do that."

The rest of the trip passed in taut silence. They dropped Carolina and the cameraman at their quarters, all of them heaving a collective sigh of relief as they drove to their base.

Mac climbed out of the vehicle, sobering on seeing the gouges in the roof of their vehicle. The path of a bullet showed clearly against the paintwork. At least the armored panels had held.

"Another day, another dollar," Garrett quipped when he saw the grooves.

"Yeah." Jeez, talk about close. She prayed she lived through her contract. If something happened to her no one would look after her father. It felt as if she stood between a rock and an inflexible wall. No choice. This was the only way she had to make quick money.

Inside, she stowed her weapon and unfastened her vest, their close call replaying in her mind. She headed for her room, closing the door behind her. Unable to remain still, she strode the length of the small room and back. The door opened without warning and Louie entered.

"Thank goodness," she muttered, taking two running steps and leaping at the same time. She needed distraction. *Now.*

Louie laughed, his arms wrapping around her shoulders and maintaining balance at the same time. Their mouths clashed, sparks shooting between them.

Clothes flew left and right as they fought to undress each other, to continue kissing and touching at the same time. Mac groaned when Louie peeled one cup of her bra away and scooped her breast upward. He lowered his head and sucked her nipple into his mouth. The hard suction of his mouth sent a reaction roaring through her.

Mac wanted to get closer, to touch his skin and feel the power in his solid muscles. She wanted to grope his sexy arse. Mac laughed at the thought.

He lifted his head. "What's so funny?"

"Hurry up and strip. Those boots need to come off before your trousers."

"As much as I like the bossy command, we don't have to do everything fast. We have plenty of time before anyone will come looking for us," Louie said.

"Yeah, but I can't grope you as well if you're wearing clothes."

"Grope me, huh? Has a nice ring to it." Grinning, he tangled his fingers in the hair at her nape and licked across the shell of her ear.

She sighed, wriggling against his erection, laughing out loud when his teeth scraped over a pulse point. "Maybe we should try the bed."

Louie snorted. "I'd love to try a bed. The bunk doesn't count as a bed. It's too bloody narrow. I'm lucky I haven't knocked myself out."

"Good point." Mac considered the bunks for a second before turning back to Louie. "We could always do a little redecorating. Mattress on the floor."

"You just want to ride me, woman."

"Damn straight. Nothing better than being in control," Mac said.

Louie nodded. "Not a bad idea, but I wanna play a little first." Raw need sizzled on his face, darkening his brown eyes to almost black.

Mac took one look and moisture gathered between her legs, desire a savage throb inside her pussy. She wanted him to fill her, to slide his cock between her legs and halt the sweet pain that filled her. Damn. She closed her eyes and swallowed, tension ramping up between them. "I need you," she said, straining against his body, rubbing against his erection, and trying to force the issue, make his patience snap.

It didn't work.

Louie ran one hand down her back, pausing to strip off her dangling bra. Heat stabbed her with his every touch, her nipples pebbling to hard, needy points.

"Pretty. I love your breasts." He stroked the underside of one, lifting the heavy globe and licking the plump curve. "You taste good."

"I'm sweaty," she protested.

"Yeah, but you smell nice." He licked a slow path around the areola then blew.

"I thought you were in a hurry."

"Nah, I never said that," he said, and she could tell by his expression nothing she said would induce him to speed. Maybe she should just enjoy the ride because if there was one thing she knew about Louie it was he was a generous lover. He liked his partner to feel good. "We have plenty of time."

"Won't everyone wonder if we don't turn up in the gym?"

"No, because you're gonna say you were so tired you fell asleep. I'm gonna say I had to do some office work, and no one is going to think anything about it because after the next mission, one or both of us will be in the gym with everyone else."

Mac gave in to the impulse to touch and stroked a hand over his bristly cheek. She grinned into his serious countenance. "If you think that will work."

"We'll make it work."

"Good. Can we get to the good stuff now?"

They stared at each other. Louie rubbed his groin against her hip, his hard erection burning through the layer of fabric still separating their bodies. "This feels pretty good to me." He closed the gap between their mouths to brush a kiss over her lips. It started off slow, growing to passionate. Desperate.

Mac struggled with the button and hook of Louie's fly, desperate to feel his entire body, to fondle his arse. He had the sexiest butt. Finally, she gave up in frustration. It was difficult to concentrate on more than one thing at once. Kissing Louie fried her brain. She tried not to think about it too much, the way he made her feel. Happy and excited.

There was no time in her life for a relationship. This *thing* with Louie was all about the sex. She tore her mouth from his. "Can we do this?"

"All in good time."

"But this isn't romance. It's fucking to scratch an itch," she snapped, glaring at him. Why wasn't he like other men? They craved sex and took what they wanted without a desire to savor the experience.

Louie stilled. Surprise then determination flitted over his face. Maybe some intrigue as well. Dammit, she didn't want to captivate him, make him want to pursue her. She wanted him to understand that this was casual, without expectations on her part. What was wrong with plain, selfish sex? The world had gone mad, becoming way too politically correct for her liking.

Louie stepped back, his gaze softening as he studied her body. "You've lost weight. You need to eat."

"You're not my mother."

Laugh wrinkles formed at the corner of his eyes. Grinning, he unfastened his trousers and slipped them and his boxer-briefs down his legs. "A fact I am truly grateful for." He reached for the mattress on the bottom bunk and lifted it onto the floor, flexing biceps attracting her attention.

In Fiji, she'd licked the flowing lines of his tribal tattoos,

81

tasted his skin and indulged herself. The fleeting idea of repeating the experience brought a frown.

After flicking the lock on the door, he strode over to her. "You're right. Let's fuck."

Although she'd used the term a few minutes earlier, the harsh word seemed to echo between them. It hurt.

Aware of the contradiction in her thinking, she forced a smile while confusion reigned inside her. Ignoring the inconsistencies in her thoughts, she let Louie seduce her. Sexy smile. Gorgeous body. It didn't take much to fall into his embrace.

His hands skimmed with purpose and the skill she'd become used to. His mouth was soft on hers, and he kissed her until desire grabbed every scrap of her attention. She shivered, feeling the weight of her breasts, the heavy expectation flooding her body. A soft, needy sound escaped, and she tilted her neck, silently asking for the redirection of his mouth.

"Not your neck." Louie kissed the slope of her breast and sucked until her inner walls clenched with need.

"More," she whispered. "I need more."

"Patience," he countered. "I told you, we have time."

He didn't intend to hurry, so she gave up and went with the flow. Skin brushed skin, and she squirmed and twisted when he tongued her breasts, stroked her arse.

He lifted her and settled her on the mattress, following her down. Things became more serious then. Heated whispers. Touches designed to inflame. Mac felt as if she floated, his touch making her want more of the erotic assault.

Louie parted her legs and lifted her hips in a smooth move. Seconds later, his mouth and tongue devoured her swollen flesh. His stubble scraped the tender skin of her inner thighs while his tongue traced wicked patterns around her clit. A moan escaped, and she bit her bottom lip to still another cry. A finger pushed inside her with a hot, easy glide. Her stomach hollowed, her hips canting to push against his tongue.

"Louie, please. I need you to fill me now. We can do it all over again. I just need you now."

Louie stilled and glanced up at her. "Promise?"

"Yes."

He nodded, the undeniable masculine interest deepening. "I know how you feel about promises."

Oops, she'd forgotten that. While they'd been in Fiji, the discussion had come up. She couldn't remember how, but she'd told Louie she never, ever went back on her word.

He pulled his finger from her and without breaking their gaze, he licked it clean. Her breath caught, her chest tightening with a wave of emotion. Even though she knew nothing could come between them because of her vow to her father, she couldn't help but wish things were different. This man, he touched places inside her...

Swallowing, she tugged him closer, sure every emotion shone on her face for him to read.

"Hey, don't you want to go on top?"

"Plain old missionary is fine for what I have in mind." Hard, hot, sweaty sex. The kind that made a woman forget her problems.

Louie didn't say anything, but he grinned, and the sight made her catch her breath again. He was stunning when he smiled, and despite her complaints, his take-charge manner didn't bother her. It was part of his military training and something she respected. Trusted. During their time in Fiji, he'd bound her with silken scarves, the loss of freedom making the sex sizzling hot. She sighed as he moved over her and slipped inside, the head of his cock barely embedded.

"Louie." Mac tried to move but he held her still.

"I wouldn't want you to think you're getting your own way."

Mac snorted. "How could I think that? This is torture. You're tormenting me." He opened his mouth as if he were going to speak but didn't. Instead, he pushed a little deeper and pulled back. In a silence thick with tension, they stared at each other.

Mac clenched her inner muscles and he groaned, pushing inside her fully with one slow, toe-curling stroke.

"I love the first, perfect stroke," she whispered. "I like the way it feels when I stretch around you."

"Feels pretty damn good on this end," Louie said with a strangled laugh.

At first, he kept the thrusts slow and steady, but she urged him on, digging her fingernails into his shoulders, kissing his neck, the whorls of a tattoo and undulating against his muscular body with sighs of sincere appreciation. There was no pretense because Louie really did it for her. Later, she'd probably think about how wrong it was to let her emotions show, about the danger to her sanity and the way he screwed with her focus and future plans. Yeah, later. Right now she intended to wring every bit of enjoyment from their encounter.

Mac met each of his thrusts while their lips met in wild abandon. His scent surrounded her, his taste filled her. She climbed higher and higher, then for one scary moment, she balanced on a knife-edge of pleasure. A moment of clarity before she soared over the precipice into ecstasy. No other word for it. Mac clutched his sweaty shoulders and hung on, savoring the lingering pulses of her sex as she sailed back down to earth.

"Louie," she whispered.

"Good?"

"Yeah." The word was a soft sigh of pleasure.

"We'll see if you can go again." His chuckle, laced with sin, made her smile. He increased his strokes, changed the angle, and to her surprise, a sweet burn flared. She melted against him, her hands busy touching as much of him as she could reach. Her hands came to rest on his muscular butt. Nice.

"Aw, damn, Joanna," he whispered hoarsely against her neck. He slammed into her with hard, digging strokes, the sounds of fucking loud and distinctive.

Mac didn't care. She felt a primal sense of satisfaction as his cock jackhammered into her and at the hunger etched on his face. He came with deep body shudders, his seed splashing into her. When he finally stilled, he rolled, laughing when they fell off the mattress onto the floor. He wrapped his arms around her and held tight. Mac knew she should move, that they should clean up, shower, and maybe hit the gym. Instead, the urge to move trotted right out of her mind, replaced by contentment. Cuddling in Louie's arms felt right, and that should have scared her half to death.

CHAPTER FIVE

FIVE DAYS LATER

Louie hit the shower early, untangling his body from Mac after another session of lovemaking. Every time they returned from a grueling day, they had sex. Most days, he admitted, although they were both careful about it. Sometimes they hit the gym first, either lifting weights, pummeling a boxing bag, or sprinting up and down the basketball court with the others. At other times, they met in their room and sweated out their stress by bumping body parts. Louie lived for those moments, and it was starting to eat him alive not being able to tell Mac how he felt.

"Hey, Louie. You're up early," Simon said.

"Yeah, couldn't sleep." Not without wanting to fuck

Mac again. Holding her close and trying not to wake her had driven him to the shower. Luckily, the cold water had done the trick before Simon arrived.

"It must be difficult rooming with Mac," Simon said.

Louie adjusted the water to warm and grabbed the soap. "It's not so bad now. After seeing the way she handles herself, it's easier to think of her as one of the guys."

"And that's why you're up so early taking a cold shower?"

Louie wanted to tell him to fuck off but knew Simon would suspect something. He needed more finesse. "Can't help being a male."

Simon snorted. It could've been a laugh. Louie wasn't a hundred percent sure on that.

"We still training this morning?" Simon stripped and turned on another shower.

Louie appreciated the change of subject. "Yeah. And a recon this afternoon. The news company wants to film out west of the city."

"Don't tell me. They want to go to the latest bombing site."

"No, they want to interview some of the villagers out there. See how they're getting on with their day-to-day lives." Louie didn't believe it for a moment. Carolina Eastern had an agenda and it involved Mac.

"But it's near the bombing site?"

"Yeah." Louie turned off the tap and grabbed his towel. After roughly drying himself, he wrapped the damp towel around his waist, scooped up his shower bag and headed back to his room.

Mac was still asleep when he entered and he tiptoed around, trying not to wake her. He'd never met a soldier like her. Just about every soldier of his acquaintance slept lightly. Not Mac. Despite being a heavy sleeper, the moment she opened her eyes she was alert and hit the ground running.

Louie dressed and powered up his laptop before checking his watch. He crouched beside Mac and resisted the urge to kiss her awake. "Mac." He shook her shoulder, and when she didn't stir, he shook her a fraction harder and raised his voice. "Mac, wakey, wakey." A third hard shake did the trick.

"Is it time to get up?"

"You have time for a shower before breakfast." Louie stood and moved over to his laptop.

With a groan, Mac rolled to her feet. She lifted her arms above her head in an unconscious stretch. Louie couldn't help enjoying the show. He cocked a hip against the desk and unabashedly stared, a smile playing around his lips. He loved her hair loose and tumbling around her shoulders.

Her breasts bore a couple of bruises, small suction marks he'd made. It gave him a sense of satisfaction, knowing they were there, hidden beneath her clothes while they went about their daily work.

Her breasts pulled to tight nubs, affected by the cooler morning air. Sleek muscles rippled as she stretched, freezing when she noticed his attention.

"Having fun?"

Louie ignored the frigid tone. "Hell yeah."

"Bastard." Mac pulled on a long T-shirt and a pair of baggy shorts. After grabbing a towel and a shower bag, she slammed from their room.

Grinning, he signed into his email account. The first email was from Nikolai. He scanned it. Nothing new there. No one Nikolai had talked to knew much about Mac, although Nikolai hoped to catch up with some of the soldiers she served with at a reunion dinner coming up later in the month. He scanned the details again and stopped at one thing he'd missed. Mac's father had been a soldier. He was still alive, but her mother had died twenty years ago. Interesting. He'd ask Nikolai to research that angle for him.

Aware of the need to hurry, Louie fired off a return email, sending his special love to Nikolai's wife, Summer, because he knew it would piss off his friend. He was very protective of his wife, but an adventurer at heart, Summer didn't make it easy for him.

Louie signed off just as Mac arrived back from her shower.

"You put love bites all over my breasts," she snarled at him. "You're lucky no one noticed but me."

"I'm sorry." Not true, but he wasn't stupid enough to admit it. He'd never acted possessive about a woman before. Until Mac. He hated the other men seeing her naked in the shower. At least he could touch when they were in private. But if Mac re-upped for another six months...

He had to change her mind. Somehow. Even though the woman handled herself better than most, he'd worry about her.

"Hell," she said in disgust. "You're not sorry at all. What is wrong with you? Do you think the others will respect me if they think we're fucking each other? They'll start watching me like I'm a bug in a jar. I'll have to prove myself all over again."

She was right. It wasn't fair, but that was the way it went. "I'm sorry. Okay? Why don't you tell them you did it when you fell yesterday?"

"If they ask questions I will, but I doubt they'll believe me."

"They will after training today," Louie said. "We have a grueling session in store. You won't be the only one with bruises by the end of the day. Do you want to check your email before I turn off the laptop? You have time if you're quick."

Mac dressed rapidly in her neutral-colored shirt and trousers. "Thanks. That would be great."

"I'll leave you to it. Power the laptop down for me once you're done." Without waiting for her reply, he left their room.

Halfway down the passage, he smelled the coffee. Most of the team was already there, plowing through a huge breakfast.

"Hey, Louie. Word is you and Mac have something going. Is that true?" one of the men called.

Shit. Louie forced a huge grin. "Aside from the fact that Mac's fiancé would likely try to gut me if I touched his woman, the lady isn't interested in me."

"And what about the bruises?"

"What bruises?" Hell, they'd noticed the bruises but hadn't said anything to Mac. Yet.

The guy gestured at his chest.

Louie turned away to pour a coffee. "No idea. She fell pretty heavy at training yesterday."

"So you didn't look?" another asked.

"Not polite," Louie said. "Like I said, she has a man. She's not interested in any of us."

"Damn straight," Mac said entering the room. "Why would I want any of you when Sam is waiting for me at home?"

"You really engaged?"

"Yep," Mac said. "Getting married soon."

"Why are you here?"

"Why are you lot so nosy?" Mac countered.

"Not much else to do." They all laughed at that.

"I'm here for the money, the same as most of you. And you do realize I'm doing you all a favor sharing with Louie? The boss snores like a freight train."

Louie grinned at the hoots, playing along. Mac wouldn't know because she slept through anything, especially after sex. He shrugged, accepting the teasing and winked at Mac on the sly. They could say what they liked about him. It was better than letting them hone their wits on her.

Mac moved up the mess line beside him, the good humor absent now that her back was to the rest of the men. When he looked closer, he noticed the faint redness of her eyes. Hell, had she been crying?

"You okay?" he asked gruffly. Like most men, crying women scared him half to death. He never knew what to do and usually ended up making things worse. Yeah, he had a healthy respect for women and tears.

"Why shouldn't I be?" The snap in her tone warned him to tread lightly.

"No reason."

"I'm fine. What time are we back from training?"

"Only a couple of hours today. Should be back by eleven at the latest."

Mac gave a clipped nod and moved away to join some of the others. Louie wanted to follow but forced himself to take a seat with Simon.

"Have you seen a photo of her fiancé?" Simon asked.

"Nah, Mac's a pretty private person."

"Don't you think that's weird? Everyone else carries a photo of their wife or kids or girlfriend. Don't you think Mac would show everyone?"

Good point, but then he knew Mac didn't have a fiancé. It was a cover to keep her fellow soldiers away. Not a bad strategy. Producing a photo would bolster her story and give it the ring of truth. Maybe a ring as well, although not many of the married security force wore rings on their fingers. "As I said, she's a private person. You want to know, you ask her. I'm not about to snoop through her things."

"So, you'd leave your room open so one of us could do the snooping?" one of the guys asked.

"Hell no," Louie said. "I didn't come down in the

last shower. That would give you free range to rummage through my stuff as well."

The banter continued throughout the meal, a way of dealing with the stress of their job. Louie kept a surreptitious eye on Mac and noticed she didn't eat much, pushing her food around her plate. Something had happened after he left the room. She'd intended to check her email, which suggested she'd received news from home. He wondered how to handle the situation. With most of his men, it was easy. He called them into his office, and they talked the problem through. Other times, his men approached him. Personal problems wreaked havoc on a soldier, taking their head out of the game. They were a team. They relied on each other. One screw up could mean loss of their VIP or that one or all of them died.

The situation with Mac was different because of their personal history. Louie scowled down at his plate. He'd play it by ear. Observe. It was the only thing he could do in the circumstances.

MISSING. HER FATHER WAS missing from the home. At some stage during the night, he'd climbed out of bed, dressed, and wandered outside. The director of the

95

nursing home had assured Mac when she'd phoned in a panic that they were searching for him and had called the police.

Mac was worried sick and couldn't do a thing from half a world away. She couldn't leave Iraq on a whim, had known it when she signed up for six months. She didn't know what to do. Somehow, she managed to get through the training session by channeling her impotent fury and sense of helplessness.

Mac worked through the training exercises with focus. A military machine. She'd scared the hell out of her team with her icy precision and concentration. A bitter laugh escaped as she strode toward their room. She hoped Louie turned up rather than heading to his office or going to the gym. Restless energy hummed through her limbs, and she couldn't keep still. She yanked the door open and did her usual pacing.

A glance at her watch told her it was the middle of the night in New Zealand. Mac powered up Louie's laptop anyway to check her email. Nothing. She fired off an email and tried not to think about her father, confused and alone in an unfamiliar part of the city.

The door flew open just as she hit send. Their eyes met and Mac's heart turned a hard somersault, slamming against her ribs. The hungry glint in his eyes, the hard mask of desire he didn't try to hide told her they wanted the same thing.

She stood, quivering, her womb clenching in a hard pulse of need, her breasts exquisitely sensitive beneath the plain cotton of her bra. Each breath was an exercise in torture.

The lock on the door turned, the click loud in the tension-filled room. With two giant steps, Louie crowded her, pushing her up against the wall, his mouth slamming down on hers. She gripped his head, melting into his chest and molding herself to his body. This was what she wanted. Hard and fast. The edge of roughness. His tongue thrusting into her mouth, his dark flavor heady and alluring.

She moaned, ripped his shirt from his trousers and slid her hands over his warm flesh. This was what she needed. Without pulling away from the kiss, she fumbled with his fly, desperate to free his cock and feel the smooth skin spearing against her belly. He winced at her feverish attempts to get off his clothes.

Louie ripped his mouth off hers. "Jesus, woman. Let me do that."

"Sorry." With Louie taking care of his clothes, she went to work on her own, bending to unlace her boots and unfasten her trousers.

Louie was ready before she'd started on her shirt and bra. He advanced, crowding her against the wall again, taking her mouth in another hard kiss. The surface was cold against her arse, the thin panties no barrier to the chill. She started when Louie roughly spread her legs, sighed when his fingers stroked across her swollen folds. A zing of pleasure shot through her, the friction of his fingers on the thin cotton a tantalizing drag over her flesh.

Not enough. Not nearly enough.

As if he read her desperation, he yanked her panties, ripping them off her body and running a questing finger the length of her cleft. He grunted at the warm arousal, thrusting one finger inside her while he unfastened the buttons of her shirt. Seconds later, he shoved her bra aside and sucked hard on one nipple.

Mac moaned, not caring who heard, merely wanting to drive away her pain and to feel instead. She arched into his touch. So good. Louie knew just how to touch her, he knew what she liked. She almost cried when he lifted his head and removed his finger. A protest built on her lips then the crown of his cock pressed at her entrance. He lifted her effortlessly, pressing her against the wall and working his way into her tight channel. She flexed around him, a needy cry bursting from between her lips. Her fingers curled into his shoulders, nails digging into his flesh.

"Too much?"

"Louie, I need you. Fuck me hard. Make it go away." She bit into the cushion of her bottom lip, aghast at her words. He'd ask questions, maybe not now but later. To her relief, he started to plunge into her body. Hard, deep strokes that made them both gasp. She shuddered, the rub of his cock against her delicate tissues almost turning her inside out. Her eyes fluttered, closed and she sank into sensation. Pleasure so good it hurt. She drowned in the desire, the building need. The bliss. Wedged between him and the wall she writhed, the delectable agony almost too much. Then the tension snapped, and she flew, falling apart in his arms, shuddering through her orgasm. Louie shafted her deep. Two more hard strokes and she felt a flood of wetness. They both stilled, breathing hard. Then Louie crushed her mouth under his before gentling the kiss and moving back. He lifted her off his cock, the resulting emptiness bringing a frown.

She wanted him again.

"You up for some more?" he asked in a gritty voice, his brown eyes dark with passion.

"Yeah." That's what she liked about Louie. He didn't make a big deal out of this, and when they were outside this bedroom, he treated her like one of the team. She liked that.

"Good." He let her slide down his body and held her until she gained her footing. Gently, he unbuttoned the rest of her shirt and reached behind her to unfasten her bra. He pinched one nipple, the sharp burst of pain bringing a thick slice of pleasure.

"I feel like we've only taken off the edge," she murmured as he yanked off her clothing. A sigh whooshed free, and she reached out to touch.

"On the bed this time," he said, capturing her hand. He led her over to the set of bunks and drew her down.

As always it was a tight fit, not that she'd complain. Close was good. Louie rolled her under him, his hot breath caressing her cheek before he kissed her. Immediately the tension amplified between them, her vagina clenching with renewed hunger. She shifted against him in silent demand, glad to feel his erection digging into her hip. Parting her legs, he slipped inside her, invading. Retreating. Wetness pooled between her thighs, along with desperate need.

Trouble. She and Louie were an accident waiting to happen. She knew it. She suspected Louie knew it too, yet she couldn't keep away. He made all the ugliness, the pain, the worry recede, even if it was only short-term. He rocked their bodies together, their lips meeting again and again in languorous kisses.

The easy glide and faint drag over her swollen clit pushed her need to urgent. She twisted her body, arching against him, feeling safe, surrounded by his masculine strength. His strokes quickened, a guttural moan filling the room as he came with a convulsive heave of muscles.

Their lovemaking perfumed the air as he softened and pulled out of her. He grinned, a rakish grin of confidence as he kissed his way down her body. He tongued a damp path around her bellybutton, an ache of emptiness filling her as she waited for his next move. His fingers tickled across her hip bone then lower, combing through the trimmed pubic hair.

The heat of his mouth shouldn't have surprised her, but it did. Mac glanced down at his broad shoulders and his dark hair as he carefully sucked on her swollen clit, bringing it back to vibrant life. A prickle of heat fired off, nerve endings leaping with joyful abandon. He took his time, handling her gently, the merest flicker of his tongue before pausing. The prickles of heat intensified, her pussy fluttering in time with her heartbeat. Her hips jerked. She pinched a nipple, tugged hard. Combined with the flicker of his tongue, the suction of his lips, it was enough to push her body into freefall. Her clit pulsed along with her vagina, the flash of heat roaring down her legs, flaring through her belly and echoing across her chest.

Slowly, she came down from the high, sighing and stretching with pleasure. Until she remembered her father.

"What's the time?"

"Two thirty-five."

Still not the time to ring the nursing home.

Louie moved up the bed and pulled her close. She knew he could feel the tension in her muscles and must wonder about the cause. With the sex they'd just had, they should both feel relaxed and limber.

"What's wrong?"

"Nothing," she said, aiming for casual. The hard expression on his face told her she hadn't pulled it off. Suspicion and questions suddenly hovered between them.

A knock on the door jolted them both.

"Yeah?" Louie called.

"Phone call for Mac." It was Simon.

"I'll be there in a few minutes," she said.

"It's from home," Simon said.

Silently Louie pulled away and climbed off the bunk. Mac rolled off and grabbed her clothes, rapidly dressing. She dragged her hands through her hair, scowled and rapidly unfastened the tight knot she'd confined it in for training.

Wordlessly, she opened the door to find Simon waiting.

He took one look at her, his eyes narrowing. She caught the faint flare of his nostrils and blushed.

"Where's the call?"

"In the mess. Tai's waiting by the phone to make sure no one else tries to use it."

Simon knew. Too late to worry now. Mac hurried to the mess and hoped none of the others realized what Simon had interrupted. The last thing she needed was gossip.

Louie grabbed his clothes and rapidly dressed. Mac had tensed when she'd heard about the phone call.

A tap on the door sounded and Louie scowled. It didn't take a genius to work out who wanted him. "Yeah?" he snarled, hoping he'd put Simon off.

"Can I come in?"

Louie snorted. Somehow he didn't think he'd be able to stop his mate. And, from the sound of it, Simon wanted to rip him a new one. He might be boss but that never stopped any of the men from giving their opinion when they thought it warranted.

"Louie?"

"Dammit, come in."

The door opened and Simon stepped inside. He wrinkled his nose but shut the door. "Smells like a whorehouse in here."

"I wouldn't know. I've never frequented one."

"You're fucking her." The harsh cast to Simon's face said it all. Despite their friendship, Simon thought he'd forced Mac into the sex somehow. He thought the worst of him.

"So much for friendship," Louie snarled. "Don't I get the benefit of the doubt?"

"If we were at home in a civilian situation it would be different," Simon said. "But we're not. We're at war where personal shit can take a person's head out of the game. One mistake over here and people die."

"I know that." Louie's icy reply didn't make Simon back down. Truth was, Simon was right to call him on their relationship. "Talk to Mac," he said finally. "Ask her about coercion."

"I intend to."

Louie sighed and dragged a hand through his short hair. What a fuckin' mess, although how he'd thought they'd manage to keep their relationship a secret with the way they all lived so close he didn't know. "Talk to Mac," he said again, walking to the door. He opened it and waited for Simon to leave.

Simon hesitated before saying, "I'll talk to Mac." The tense set of his face and shoulders told Louie the rest. If he didn't like what he heard he'd make noise with the management. Female recruits were a rarity, and this situation hadn't come up before.

Louie sighed. If there was trouble, he'd deal with it. Maybe they could turn his office into an extra bedroom. His hands clenched to fists at his sides. He sure as hell wasn't going to let Mac room with any of the others.

Simon opened his mouth to say something else and closed it again, his face hard and expressionless. He left and Louie closed the door with a moody slam. He didn't want things to change. He didn't want Mac to move to another room. She was his pressure valve, releasing the stress that built inside. He sighed again then shook his head with a rueful grin.

When he'd arrived in Fiji, he'd suffered from tension headaches and every noise made him jump. One look at Joanna had changed everything. He'd made his move, cutting off the attentions of a cocky Australian with determination. From that first night they'd been inseparable, sharing a bed every night and every waking moment. It had been bloody hard parting from her, and he'd tried to contact her almost straightaway. He could hardly blame her for giving him false details given the circumstances, not when he'd done the same.

Louie straightened the room, smoothing the bunk bed and picking up the tattered remnants of her panties. His hand closed around them, squeezing tightly. He couldn't do it. No way did he intend to let Joanna escape again.

MAC PICKED UP THE phone with a trembling hand, her stomach bucking with more terror than she felt facing insurgents on the streets of Iraq.

"Mac McGregor," she said.

"This is Director Jones-Black. I'm ringing about your father."

"Have you found him?" Mac broke in impatiently, not willing to wait for the man to get to the point. "Is my father okay?"

"The police have found him and are bringing him back to the home. They've assured me he's all right, but our onsite medical staff will monitor his health on his return."

Mac's legs shook so much she sank to the floor. Tears flooded into her eyes, and she swiped them away with a touch of impatience. As her father always said, soldiers don't cry. "What's the time there in New Zealand?" she asked, unable to make the time calculation with her mind still in turmoil.

"It's two in the morning."

"Thanks. I'll ring later today to check on my father."

"Don't worry, Ms. McGregor. We'll watch him closely

so this situation doesn't happen again." The stern tone told Mac he meant what he said and didn't take a missing resident lightly. It reinforced the impression she'd received when she first met him and went a long way to soothing her tension.

"Thanks. I'll call in a few hours." Mac replaced the phone and hugged her knees, hiding her face for an instant. Her heart thudded as if she'd run a hundred-meter sprint.

"You okay?"

Mac jerked her head up and swiped the back of her hand over her nose. "Simon."

Simon crouched beside her, an expression of concern in his blue eyes. He was so close she could see the individual sandy eyelashes and the bristles of his stubble.

"I'm fine."

Simon looked over his shoulder. Mac followed his gaze and saw several of their teammates watching them. Simon stood and extended his hand to her.

"We can't talk here. Come to my room. We have time before we go out on recon to prepare for tomorrow."

Mac accepted his hand and stood. She silently followed, knowing this was about her and Louie. She thought rapidly and admitted the truth. She liked what she and Louie had now—a sort of friends-with-benefits deal. When they were out on recon or looking after a VIP, Louie treated her like one of the others, just what she expected, and she liked it that way. No, she didn't want a change.

Simon opened the door to his room, stuck his head inside then stood aside for her to enter. He closed the door and turned to face her. "What's up with you and Louie? Did he force you to have sex?"

Mac's mouth dropped open in astonishment. "No way," she said. "Of course not. Louie isn't like that."

"Then what's going on?"

Mac thought rapidly and wondered about going with the truth. It was always the simplest way. "Is this in confidence? You won't tell anyone?"

"It depends," Simon said. "If I think it's going to affect morale or cause problems on a job, I can't promise not to take this further."

"Fair enough." She wouldn't keep quiet either if she thought emotions would make one of their team screw up. A slow breath eased from her as she considered where to start, how much to tell Simon. A quick look at his tense shoulders and determined face told her not to lie, which left her with a version of the truth. "I met Louie when I was on holiday in Fiji. We hit it off and became...close." Heat suffused her cheeks and she focused on her clasped hands instead of watching his face. "I didn't know Louie was here. It was a shock to both of us."

"So, you didn't keep in contact?"

"No. It's hard to maintain any sort of relationship when you're in the military. I told Louie I was a secretary. He wasn't exactly forthcoming about his background either."

Simon's mouth twisted. "I see."

She risked a quick glance at him, her heart knocking against her ribs with sudden alarm. Simon saw more than she was comfortable with, and Mac hoped like hell she had her game face firmly intact. "We're friends," she said decisively. "That's all. The sex helps both of us. It takes off the edge after a stressful day. And that's all it is—sex. What we do in private is no one's business but ours, especially since we're totally professional in public. We're both aware we're part of a team. We want to make it through our contracts in one piece, just the same as you and the others." This time Mac spoke directly to Simon and didn't hide. Her voice rang with truth, even if the snarky part of her hidden deep inside sneered from the sidelines and told her she was spouting rubbish. A big fat lie. If it wasn't for her father, she'd be considering the future and wondering if Louie could play a part in her life.

"Are you sure there's nothing except casual sex involved?"

Her stomach plummeted but she managed to frown at Simon. A short laugh escaped. "We're strictly friends

109

with benefits. Nothing more. We both know and accept that once our contracts are over we'll go our separate ways. Louie did not force me to have sex with him. It was a mutual decision that we discussed first before taking action. Okay? Have I answered all your questions?"

"Yes. I'm not going to say anything unless I think your friends-with-benefits deal is causing trouble out on the field."

Relief whispered through Mac, making her realize how tense the discussion had made her. Struggling through lies and half-truths would do that to a person. "Thank you."

Simon checked his watch. "We'd better move it. We're leaving on the recon in fifteen minutes."

Mac nodded and left Simon's room, coming face-to-face with Tai. His eyes rounded in surprise before a sly grin spread across his face.

"Don't tell me. You were practicing your map reading together."

"No, I had a problem and needed someone to talk with," Mac said. "Oh, for God's sake. Take that look off your face. Simon's married. If you think I'd fool around with Simon or any of you here, you've got rocks in your head! I have much better taste." She stomped off, fury pumping through her body. She ignored the two men who had exited their rooms and overheard her tirade.

Mac burst into their room to find Louie waiting for her. One searching look from him added fuel to the fire. "What is it with you men? You're like a pack of old women with your gossip."

"What happened?"

"I talked with Simon or rather he questioned our motives. Then Tai caught me coming out of Simon's room and implied we had something going on together."

"I'll fix it," Louie said.

"No, you won't fix it because I've already told him exactly what I thought of his stupid idea. Honestly, all I want to do is my job." She grabbed her brush and yanked it through her hair before fastening it in a knot. With her hair restrained, some of her control returned. Donning her protective vest and picking up her weapon of choice gave her a sense of direction again. Soldier. Mercenary. That's who she was. Woman came a long way down the list.

CHAPTER SIX

THE LINE OF BRITISH army vehicles ahead of them drove at a steady pace. Mac tried to concentrate on their surroundings, the job at hand, but her mind kept returning to her father. She'd never felt such a sense of helplessness. Thank God he was safe now. Mac caught a flash of movement in her peripheral vision. Her gaze snapped to the spot. Nothing. She blinked and continued to scan the buildings, the road. Without warning a huge explosion rocked their vehicle. Mac slammed against the door. Someone cursed. A groan escaped, and her head rang from the contact with the window.

Their driver jammed on the brakes. The vehicle screeched to a stop, the fender scraping against the rear of the Jeep in front.

"IED," Louie snapped. "Ambush."

Improvised explosive device. Mac froze, every sense hyperalert. Fear swelled in her stomach. Thick black smoke shrouded vision. A loud crash made them all jump. Curse. Something thumped to the ground beside their vehicle.

"What the fuck was that?" Garrett spoke for all of them.

Mac peered through the smoke. *A body*. Shit. The blood...the gore... She battled nausea. "A soldier," she said, swallowing rapidly. IEDs killed a lot of soldiers and innocents. "Dead."

"Keep alert," Louie ordered.

A RPG struck not far from their vehicle. The soldiers in the Jeep in front of them returned fire.

"Looks like we're gonna see some action," Garrett muttered.

"Return fire," Louie ordered. "Cover the soldiers while they aid the injured."

Mac slid from their vehicle, taking refuge behind the door. She fired on instinct, her training kicking in. Take out the snipers. Fire. Fire. *Fire!*

Mac kept firing. Men cried out in pain, calling for their loved ones. She blocked out the cries, concentrating on giving the soldiers cover so they could rescue their downed comrades.

Air backup arrived and gradually the small arms fire and

RPGs trailed off. Mac swiped a grimy hand across her face, recoiling when she saw another body lying a few feet from them. Someone's sweetheart. Maybe a brother and a father. A husband. Her eyes started to sting, and she blinked rapidly to head off her tears.

"Everyone okay?" Louie asked.

"We need Garrett back here," Simon said. "Tai's hit again."

"Man's a bullet magnet," Louie muttered.

Garrett cracked a sick joke, and Mac laughed along with the others. A survival mechanism for them all.

The call to prayer sounded as they arrived back at base. They were later than usual, the night-vision goggles they donned turning the night a weird green color. At least they were safe and in one piece. Louie sighed as he made his way back to their room. Maybe he'd shift the teams around and put Mac with Simon. It would make Simon happier, and the move wouldn't cause comment amongst the rest of the men because he swapped personnel on a regular basis. Perhaps he'd talk to Mac first. See what she thought. Think about it a bit more.

Mac was in their room when he arrived, tugging off her vest. Heat and sweat made her cotton shirt mold to her chest. Louie tried not to look at her outlined breasts too much, tried not to think about how her silky skin felt when he touched her.

"I have to make a phone call," she said, her voice abrupt.

"Okay." Instinctively Louie knew sex wasn't in the cards. "I feel like playing some basketball. I'm heading to the gym as soon as I take care of a couple of admin things. You going to the gym after your phone call?"

She hesitated before nodding. "Yeah, a game of basketball sounds great. If the others don't want to play I'll whip your butt playing one-on-one."

Louie grinned. "You can try. How about the loser gives the winner a backrub?" He knew she was a sucker for a backrub and no matter how the game played out he'd be a winner. His hands on her or her hands on him. Yep, a winner either way.

"Deal." She left in a hurry, making him curious about the phone call.

At least she didn't seem upset about Simon poking his nose into their affairs. Louie thought about questioning Simon then decided against it. He didn't want to give Simon an inkling of what he felt for Mac. That really would worry his friend. No, best he play things carefully and work on hooking Mac with patience and stealth.

MAC DIALED THE HOME where her father resided. Despite the director's assurances she wanted to talk to her father. Reassure herself. If her father would consent to take the call. These days he lived in the past. An active soldier. Each day was a new mission.

The call connected, and the director picked up.

"Ah yes. Ms. McGregor, I've been expecting your call."

"Is my father okay?"

"He's fine. After our last call, he's had a sleep. I thought you might want to speak to him, so after he woke, he's been helping the office staff with some small chores."

"Thank you," Mac said, touched at the director's thoughtfulness. Although he came across as fussy and officious, every person she'd spoken to had given the home glowing references. She wanted the best for her father, no matter what the cost. "Did you find out where my father went? How he was able to wander away?"

"Mr. McGregor said he was on a recon mission," the director said. "He sneaked from his room and managed to get past the security man at the front gate."

Mac suppressed a smile. "Oh."

"He's convinced the new people at the farm up the road are doing something illegal," the director added.

That didn't sound good. She knew how tenacious her father became once an idea popped into his head. He'd only consented to go to the home because he thought it was a barracks. He'd approved of the sentry on the gate.

"I'll try to talk to him." Mac would speak to him, but she didn't think he'd listen. Maybe she could give him a new mission. That might work although she'd have to get one of the men to issue his new orders. Her father came from the old school. Mac knew he was proud of her accomplishments, but his Alzheimer's disease had propelled him backward to a time where women kissed their husbands and boyfriends goodbye before the men went off to war. Females kept the home fires burning. They didn't fight wars on the front.

"I'd appreciate that, Ms. McGregor." This time the director's voice held a trace of bite. "We can't have your father disrupting our routine. He must learn to stay within the vicinity where we can care for him."

"I'll tell him." A sliver of fear crept through Mac. The home had to work for her father, at least for the months until her contract expired.

"One moment. I'll get your father to come to the phone."

Mac turned to lean against the wall and wondered if she should purchase a cell phone despite the extra cost. But the area was relatively private, everyone keeping clear when someone used the phone. She stared across the room, her gaze connecting with Louie's. Immediately warmth suffused her body. Awareness. She smiled at him, only looking away when someone picked up the phone.

"Your father refuses to come to the phone," the director said in clear exasperation.

"Tell him I have his new orders for him," Mac said.

A harsh sigh echoed down the line. "Very well."

"You have new orders, Sir?" Her father's crisp voice came down the line. A lump lodged in her throat. He sounded so alert. Healthy even.

"Yes, soldier. I have new orders. I want you to listen closely."

"With respect, I will not take orders from a secretary," her father said.

Damn. She glanced across the room, saw Louie, and came to a quick decision. She had to do something. "One moment. I will get the lieutenant for you."

She put the phone down and stepped away.

"Are you finished?" one of the men asked.

"No, sorry. I need Louie for a sec. Can you get him for me please?"

"Sure."

Mac waited, her heart pounding. She didn't want this but her options were limited. It would take time to arrange for someone else to phone the orders through. More questions she didn't want to answer. Louie would do this for her.

"Is something wrong?"

Without looking at him, she said, "My father is in a home. He has Alzheimer's and thinks he's still a soldier. I need a lieutenant to tell him you're aware of the situation and that he should stay at the home to await further orders. Tell him it could be a few months before you are ready to take out the target." She tensed, waiting for questions. They didn't come.

Louie took the phone from her, squeezed her shoulder gently with his free hand and started to speak. "Lieutenant Lithgow here. Is this McGregor?" He paused, his gaze on Mac as he listened. "Good. Good job, soldier. We're aware of the situation. They're under surveillance while we gather evidence. I need you to patrol the grounds to make sure the enemy doesn't infiltrate your residence. Keep the others safe. The mission will take several months, soldier," Louie said crisply. "Patrol each day until I contact you with further orders. Clear, soldier?" Louie paused again. "Yes, that's right soldier. I'll be in contact." He handed the phone back to Mac. His eyes darkened, and she fancied she saw a flicker of compassion, but it disappeared before she could be sure.

"Thank you," she whispered.

Louie nodded and strode away. Mac watched until he disappeared from sight. She knew he'd have questions. Questions she didn't want to answer, despite owing him.

"Are you there, soldier?" Mac relaxed when she heard her father's even breathing. "Do you accept your orders?"

"Yes, ma'am. I won't let the lieutenant down."

The buildup of tears finally overflowed, and one trickled down her cheek. "Good. Take care, soldier. I'd like to talk to the director." Mac waited while her father handed over the phone. It hurt knowing her father didn't recognize her any longer. She swallowed, the lump in her throat so big she wondered if she'd manage to speak to the director.

"Ms. McGregor? What did you do? He's gone off to patrol the grounds."

"I had one of my friends give him orders to stay at the home to protect the residents and to patrol the grounds while awaiting new orders. Hopefully, that should do the trick and keep him on the grounds."

"I'll contact you if I have any more problems."

"Thank you," Mac said. After goodbyes, she hung up and waved at the man waiting his turn. All she could do was wait and hope her father obeyed his orders.

AFTER THE PHONE CALL, Louie went straight to his office. Alzheimer's. God, that explained a few of the questions he'd had about her background.

His phone rang and he picked it up, his mind still on Mac.

"Carolina Eastern wants what?" he demanded, needing his boss to repeat it for him. He listened before exploding. "Mac is one person. How the hell can we protect our VIP with only Mac allowed into the woman's residence? Hell yeah. I know men aren't allowed to see the women unveiled. I know that. How is Eastern going to film the interview? She's filming?" Louie dragged a hand through his hair, his gut bouncing with misgivings. Fuck, he'd hoped Eastern would change her mind.

His boss cut through his horrified thoughts. "She's offering more money than usual to compensate for the extra danger."

"Money's no fuckin' good if you're dead," Louie growled.

"But you'll put the proposition to Mac?"

"Yeah. Yeah, I'll ask her."

"Eastern wants a decision by tomorrow. She needs to start organizing her interviews."

"Do you have any idea of the areas she has in mind?"

"Two are in the recently bombed village on the outskirts

of the city and the other is in an apartment building, near the mosque that was bombed by the Americans during fighting last month."

"Yeah, okay. I'll study the possible routes we can take so we can hit the ground running if we get the go-ahead." Louie replaced the phone, a heavy lead lump in his belly. What was Carolina Eastern thinking? This was a bad idea. A very bad idea.

A glance at his watch told him it was almost dinnertime and he'd forgotten about his challenge to take Mac on at one-on-one.

He checked their room first and when he didn't find her there, he changed into shorts and a tank top and strode to the gym. Mac was there, shooting hoops. He stopped in the doorway and watched. She bounced the ball several times then shot. The ball sailed through the hoop with a swish of net.

"Good shot," he said.

"I thought I was going to win by default." Mac's gaze was wary as she turned to look at him.

"I had to take a phone call from the boss about an upcoming assignment."

Mac's brows rose. "Something exciting?"

"I thought we were playing basketball?"

Relief flitted across her face, and Louie knew she didn't

want to talk about the phone call to her father. Too bad. They *would* talk later.

"You go first." He'd watched her play basketball, knew she was good. But he was no slouch and confident in his own abilities.

Mac grinned, bounced the ball twice and started toward him. At the last moment, she feinted left and went right, leaving him scrambling to keep up with her. Too confident obviously. With a jump, Mac shot and the ball sailed cleanly through the net.

"See if you can beat that." Her smirk fueled his determination.

He shoved his way down the court with speed and brute force, doing a lay-up and whooping when he scored.

"First to twelve," she said, catching the ball when he bounced it to her.

"Deal."

The two were evenly matched, despite their difference in height. She made up for the lack of inches with speed and a wicked shot. Mac nailed goals from all over the court.

"Six-eight to me," she taunted, her backside rolling with the swagger in her step as she strolled back from shooting another hoop.

Blood pooled in his groin, and Louie's eyes narrowed. She'd done that on purpose. Two could play that game.

Mac set off again, bouncing the ball, spinning out of his way. Louie kept pace with her, purposely jostling Mac, sliding against her sweaty body and knocking her off her feet. They fell in a tangle of limbs, chests mashing together with seductive friction.

"Sorry." Louie savored the warmth of her choppy breaths against the side of his neck, the scent of soap and clean sweat on her body. Their sticky limbs slid together, his muscular thigh rubbing between her legs as he attempted to lever off her.

Her soft gasp let him know he'd managed to rattle her. Suppressing his grin of victory, he stood, stretching out his hand to help her climb to her feet. He ran for the ball and lobbed it at the hoop before she could make a move.

"That's cheating."

"Yeah?"

"Yes," she said firmly, her eyes narrowing at his smirk.

"Is it me or is it hot in here?" Without waiting for her answer, he whipped his tank top over his head and scooped up the ball to pass to her. He caught her eyeing his arse and wanted to cheer. Now all he had to do was sink the goals to win.

Mac tipped back her head, her tongue flickering out to moisten her lips. Louie almost groaned aloud, recalling only too well how her mouth felt cruising across his body, how it looked stretched around his cock with her tongue driving him crazy. Sweat stuck her T-shirt to her chest and back, highlighting her breasts and her slim, muscular strength. In the past, soft, curved women had captured his attention. Thinking back he didn't know why. There was something very sexy about toned, strong muscles coupled with femininity, a soldier who knew how to protect herself. Louie knew Mac would threaten some men. Not him.

A feminine laugh pierced his thoughts seconds after she flitted past him and shot for goal. The ball hit the backboard and dropped through the net.

"Score! One more and you owe me a backrub."

"Bragging isn't an attractive quality."

"Do tell," she purred, closing one eye in a saucy wink as she passed the ball to him.

Louie dribbled the ball, feinting left. She read him easily, crowding him. Her scent and proximity diverted his focus, and she stole the ball, darting from him and sinking the goal before he could blink.

"And she scores again," she gloated, holding her hands above her head, and rocking her hips in a sassy dance of victory. Her breasts rose and fell rapidly, each breath still pounding through her with the exertion.

He loved seeing her carefree and happy like this, her lithe

body restless and full of energy. It made him think of Fiji. It made him think of sex. Louie cursed under his breath. Doomed. He was fuckin' doomed and it was about time he admitted this truth.

"You owe me a backrub." Her eyes sparkled with pleasure at the win, a big improvement on when he'd seen her earlier.

"Claim it whenever you want." As far as he could see, there were no losers in this competition. He got to touch her silky skin. A grin crawled across his face, and he'd take a bet on it appearing predatory. He thought he might add a few conditions of his own. This backrub would be a naked one because he believed in doing a job right. Hell, he'd make it an all-over body rub if she wanted. If she'd let him. "Ready to hit the showers?"

"Good idea. I could do with some food." She checked her watch. "We'd better hurry or we'll miss out."

They collected their gear and went to take a shower. For once there was no one else present. Louie thought about locking the door or bracing it with a chair to keep everyone out. Tempting, but he knew it could raise questions. It was bad enough having Simon pass judgment. Louie reined in his lust and told himself he only had to last through dinner then he could head to their room. As soon as Mac joined him there, the games could begin. His cock stirred at the thought, and he didn't even try to hide his erection from her when he stripped off in the shower.

She glanced at his chest, her eyes lingering on his tattoos before her gaze darted downward. His cock lengthened under her stare, and he had to fight to maintain control, to keep the groan building in his throat locked down tight.

"What are you going to do with that?" she asked.

His abrupt laugh echoed in the shower block, and he flicked on a tap, stepping under the lukewarm water. "I know what I'd like to do with it."

She glanced at the door and, grinning playfully, stepped under the same showerhead as him, jostling their bodies together. Louie didn't think. He reached for her, sliding his hands over her water-slicked back and coming to rest on her tightly muscled arse. He dipped his head and licked across the full curve of one breast.

"Louie." Shivering, she pressed closer, trapping his erection between their bodies.

"We shouldn't be doing this," he whispered, raising his head to nibble at the column of her throat.

"I know. " She grasped his shoulders and leaned up to kiss him, nipping sharply at his bottom lip. He jerked at both the bite of pain and the jolt of lust that speared to his groin. "Maybe if we make it quick," she suggested, licking her lip and sending another look at the closed door.

"It's dangerous."

"Life's dangerous," she countered, her smile slipping to reveal a vulnerability that tore at him. Hell, he knew that more than anyone. Either of them could die at any moment. No guarantees in this war.

Bending his head, he sucked a nipple into his mouth, silently signaling his surrender. If she wanted to take the risk, then so did he. She moaned quietly, tipping her head to the side, her eyes fluttering closed.

"As much as I like that, this needs to be a quickie," she said. "I'm ready. You won't hurt me."

Louie liked foreplay and exploring a woman's body as much as the next man, any sensible man, but the idea of taking appealed to him right now. His dick ached, hard enough to hammer nails already. Danger did it for him, the adrenaline rush. He reached between her legs, wanting to groan at the welcoming sweetness, so hot her juices singed his fingers. With easy strength, he lifted her. She parted her legs, and he guided his cock to her entrance. She sank down, impaling herself on his shaft.

The look on her face about killed him, the open pleasure and enjoyment, her soft sigh. His legs trembled as she gripped his shoulders and used her strength to move, the water still spraying over them. She set a steady pace, the risk of discovery aiding their speed. Her silken sheath clutched his cock, the snug fit sending an orgasmic buzz speeding through his veins.

He clutched her hips and slammed into her, their mouths meeting in an urgent, hot and wet kiss.

"Louie," she muttered, her pussy pulsing around his cock. She gasped, her eyes screwed shut, her face painted with pleasure. Hungry noises of desire escaped her parted lips, encouraging him to come.

That was all it took. The tight grasp of her body, a whisper of pleasure, and he felt the rush of semen up his cock. He exploded inside her, the rhythmic spurts just about turning him inside out. He was surprised his legs continued to hold them both upright because they felt as steady as a newborn colt's.

Aware anyone could catch them in the act at any time, Louie lifted her free of his spent cock and let her slide down his body to gain her footing. Gripping his shoulders, she stood on tiptoe and kissed him, the gentle suction of her mouth bringing renewed life to his dick. Damn, all she needed to do was touch him and he was toast.

Laughing softly, she flicked the head of his cock hard enough to make him wince. "One-track mind."

"Your fault," he said.

Mac turned away to grab her soap and turned the adjacent shower on, soaping her chest.

The shower door flew open, and Louie's blooming erection wilted a fraction. Damn, that had been close. He ducked his head under the spray of the shower, unable to look at Mac, but he angled his body slightly to block Simon's view.

"You're going to miss dinner if you don't hurry," Simon said.

"Won't be long," Mac called. "We played basketball and lost track of the time. I beat him," she added with a trace of smugness.

"Damn, woman," Louie said, suppressing a grin. "We'll be five minutes tops."

Although Simon's face bore suspicion, he didn't say anything. "I'll grab you some food if they start packing up before you get to the mess room."

"Thanks," Mac called, and started briskly shampooing her hair.

"Can I use your soap?"

"Don't you mind smelling like flowers?" Mac asked.

"Quit teasing. Your soap doesn't smell girlie, and you know it."

Grinning, she handed over her soap, and he washed his body.

It was ten minutes later when they made it to the mess. Food was still available, and they grabbed plates.

Their arrival in the mess room was a dose of reality for Louie. He had to talk to Mac about the assignment with Carolina Eastern and he hoped Mac would tell him about her father. He deserved answers after the phone call.

"I'm starving." Mac smirked at him, sweeping a lock of wet hair from her face. "I guess beating a guy at basketball will do that."

Louie growled, baring his teeth. "We could always go double or nothing."

She paused, appearing to consider the idea before nodding. "Yeah, we could do that." She leaned forward to whisper. "A girl can never have too many backrubs."

Her skin looked flushed and dewy after her shower and all he could think of was crushing her mouth under his. Hell, make that her entire body while he shafted her deep. Yeah, sounded like a plan. He shifted on his chair, ignoring the signals of approval from his body to shovel in a mouthful of mashed potatoes.

"The assignment for tomorrow going ahead?" Simon asked.

Louie looked up to meet his steely gaze and swallowed his potatoes. "Yeah. We might have another assignment—a special one. I need to talk to Mac about it because she'd take a major part of the security responsibility if we go ahead."

"Eastern," Simon growled.

"Let us eat our meal without danger of indigestion," Louie said, in a bad attempt to change the subject. He hated the idea of this assignment. His gut didn't like it because Mac would be on her own. That wasn't good, no matter which way he looked at it.

Chapter Seven

"Carolina Eastern wants me to escort her into the homes of local women and protect her while she's interviewing them?"

"Yes," Louie said. "She is willing to pay extra and since you'll be the one on the line, the boss said they'd pass that on to you. It's entirely up to you whether we go ahead or not."

"But anyone could be inside the house. We could both be shot before anyone could back me up," Mac said.

Louie nodded, knowing it was the truth.

"How much extra money is she offering?"

"Five thousand for each interview she conducts."

Mac frowned at him. "That's a lot of money."

"Yes, it is, but the money won't do you any good if you're

dead."

"I know that. I'm not stupid."

"I never said you were." Louie tried to ignore the hurt inside, knowing it wasn't personal. "Maybe you should tell me about your father."

"He has Alzheimer's. I told you that."

"Is he the reason you're here in Iraq?"

Mac sighed and all the fight went out of her. "I love him so much. After my mother left us, he was father and mother to me. My mother died a few years later. He kept me with him as much as he could and arranged for a friend's wife to look after me when he had to go away on missions. It's killing me to see him the way he is now when he always used to be so strong and robust."

"Mac, you should have said something."

"Why? You can't do anything. Nothing will make him better."

"I know that, but I could have listened if you wanted to talk. What happened? Why did I have to give him orders?"

"He's fixated on the new people who have moved in down the road from the nursing home. He thinks they're conducting an illegal operation."

"And are they?"

"Of course not. The director of the rest home assures me they're grape growers and starting to make their own wine.

There's nothing sinister about that."

No, there wasn't. Louie felt Mac's frustration. It was easy to see the way her father's health and her job tore at her.

"I didn't have the money to keep him in the home, not if I stayed with the army. That's why I made the decision to go into private security work. If I can stay alive it's a way to make quick money."

"That's what most of us are here for," Louie agreed.

"Do you know the areas Carolina Eastern intends to go to and the women she wants to visit?"

"No full particulars yet."

Mac turned away from him, striding across the bedroom floor before spinning back to face him. "Get a list from her, more details and I'll go from there. I have to admit the money is a good incentive."

Louie wanted to protest. He wanted to grab Mac and take her far away from this war. He did neither. Mac was right. It made sense to check out the offer fully before turning it down even if the thought of something happening to her about killed him. "I'll do that. Fancy some poker with the rest of the boys?"

"Yeah. Good idea. I'm too antsy to sleep."

"I'll do it," Mac said the next morning after Louie had gone through the details of the proposed sorties Carolina Eastern had sent over.

"It's dangerous."

It was easy to see Louie didn't want her to go ahead with the new assignment. She wasn't exactly thrilled either, knowing all the things that could go wrong, but the money was too good to turn down. If she could make it through this, her finances would be in good shape for a while. "Yeah, I know."

"What happens if you die? What will happen to your father?"

Shock made her gasp before anger took over. "That's low, Louie."

"Someone has to make you see sense." The expression on his face said he wasn't sorry and would do it again if that's what it took to persuade her to reject the assignment. He cared about her, and that tamped her fury down a notch. No one had cared before, apart from her father.

Mac swallowed her fury and glared at him. "If I die the insurance will cover my father for as long as he needs it, but you can bet I'll be trying to stay alive."

Louie shrugged. "Shit happens. Do you have other family to take care of your father?"

"A few cousins." No one close and it worried her.

"Look, Louie. You're not going to change my mind. Under the circumstances, I can't afford to turn down the extra money. Why don't we arrange a meeting with Carolina Eastern and try to eliminate as many of the dangers as we can. None of you can come into the buildings with me, but we can still watch the outside. I'll have radio contact. If it all goes south, you can bet I'll let you know."

"It won't be fast enough. Both you and Carolina will be dead before we can get to you."

"I agree. That's why we need to put Carolina on our schedule. I don't think all the interviews should take place in the same week. It's too predictable."

Louie nodded, glancing at the notes they had regarding the places she wanted to visit. "If you did this one first because there are more known insurgents in this area that might work." He tapped his pen on the paper, a scowl on his face. "What do you think, Simon?"

Simon, who had remained silent up until now, shook his head. "I'm with Louie on this, Mac. It's bloody dangerous and asking for trouble."

"Done deal," Mac said with a trace of impatience. "Help me make it through this and keep Carolina Eastern safe."

"Fuck, Eastern," Louie growled. "It's you we want to keep safe." For an instant open emotion blazed on his face before his features blanked to soldier.

"I'm with Louie. Eastern and her bosses might pay the bills but they're secondary. All of us want you to make it through this."

Mac swallowed while the sheen of tears formed in her eyes. She couldn't believe how easily she fit in here. They truly were like a huge family, and if one of them became injured, it hurt the rest of the team. She swallowed again and said, "Okay. Let's do that. We'll send back our conditions and see what they say."

AFTER DOING TWO RECON drives, Louie felt they were ready for the real thing. Carolina Eastern bitched and moaned the entire time, protesting they were being too cautious. The insurgents had been quiet recently, the city going through an unusual period of calm.

Nerves jumped inside Louie as they drove along the route they'd chosen, heading for an apartment block. Two women walked along the road, carrying their shopping, and a group of children played behind a wire fence in between their school lessons.

Although it was still early, the street near the market thronged with locals taking advantage of the lack of military action to purchase food and other essentials.

"Can't we go any faster?" Carolina demanded.

"No, we can't," Mac said before Louie could formulate a reply. "We have our procedures for a reason. It's to keep us alive."

Carolina sighed loudly but stopped her grumbling.

And so she should. Despite the network paying extra, it didn't mean they had to jump whenever Carolina ordered. Louie scanned the road outside the car, tensing when he saw the mobile roadblock up ahead. Their driver slowed.

"Tell them we're going to the west of the city," Louie said.

A shot rang out over to their right, and the tension in their vehicle heightened.

"Can you see what's going on?" Mac whispered.

The local soldiers waved them on and went running in the direction of the disturbance. A volley of shots fired, and their driver put his foot down, barreling away to their destination.

"How's it look?" Simon asked ten minutes later, his voice crackling over the radio.

Their driver pulled up outside the apartment building.

"Carolina, wait in the vehicle until we've checked the vicinity," Louie ordered. "Do not move until I give you the say-so."

Mac and Tai slipped from the vehicle, guns at the

ready, eyes narrowed watching for any hint of danger, any person—man, woman, or child—appearing out of place.

Louie shoved back his concern for Mac and concentrated on the job at hand. The best way to protect her was to watch her back, to do everything in his power to keep her safe. *His woman.*

A snort emerged. If he said that aloud to Mac, she'd probably deck him. Too bad. Now that he'd found her again, he didn't intend to let her flee again.

His radio crackled. "All clear."

"All clear here. We'll move Carolina inside now," Louie replied, already striding to their vehicle. He tapped on the window and with the jerk of his thumb indicated to Carolina she could leave the vehicle. She grabbed her briefcase and slid from the rear.

"Move it," Mac snapped. "We don't want to give a shooter a target."

"I know the drill," Carolina said, increasing her pace despite the snap in her voice.

Louie and Simon were right. The reporter came across as a bitch, although Mac had to give her points for tenacity. She worked to get her stories, doing everything in her power to make them happen.

"Good," Mac said, running in front of Carolina, weapon at the ready.

"Clear inside," Simon said.

Mac gave a clipped nod and followed Simon up the stairs to the first floor apartment they intended to visit. Carolina followed her with Charlie, another of their group, riding her butt.

According to their plan, Louie, Tai and Garrett waited outside at the entrance, alert for any incoming danger.

At the doorway to the apartment, they paused. Carolina was fit, Mac would give her that. After the run to the entrance and the hurried trip up the stairs, she wasn't even breathing hard.

"Are you ready?" Mac asked.

"Yes," Carolina said, smoothing a short lock of blonde hair off her face. "One thing, I promised the wife there wouldn't be any guns." Not a flicker of guilt showed on her face.

"You might have mentioned that earlier," Simon snarled at her.

"I knew you wouldn't have agreed." Carolina didn't show the slightest remorse.

"That's it. We're pulling out," Simon said.

"You can't. We're here. All the arrangements are made," Carolina said, anger coloring her cheeks.

"But you didn't pass on all the details," Simon snapped.

Carolina squeezed past Simon and thumped on the

door. "I'm going inside. The network pays your team to protect me, so you'd better do your job."

Mac inclined her head, indicating to Simon it was okay. She slid her gun into the waistband of her trousers, making sure it was out of sight. "Let's do this. Half an hour, right?"

"The interview might run longer," Carolina said.

"No, it won't," Simon said. "If Mac has to drag you out, she has orders to do it."

Carolina sent her a contemptuous glance. "I'd like to see her try."

Mac laughed inwardly and lifted her shoulders in a shrug. The door opened, and they all went on alert, prepared for anything. Mac grabbed Carolina and shoved her behind her. The two men pulled back a fraction so they were out of the line of sight, but their weapons were ready should they be required.

"Reporter for the interview," Mac said.

The woman nodded and opened the door wider. With adrenaline pumping through her body, she stepped inside the small apartment. It was spotlessly clean with the scent of cinnamon and cloves perfuming the air.

Two other women sat watching her and Carolina, their dark eyes curious as they inspected them. In the corner of the room, a baby fussed and one of the women rose to attend to it. In another room, a woman sang. She sounded young. The ring of a phone interrupted the singing.

"My daughter. Her friends are always ringing," the woman who answered the door said with a smile.

Mac relaxed a fraction. If danger lurked inside this apartment, it wasn't in plain sight. "Half an hour," she murmured to Carolina. "Clock is ticking."

Carolina's mouth tightened, firming to a flat line, but she smiled at the woman who had answered the door. "I'm Carolina Eastern."

Mac's cue to blend into the wallpaper. She stood with her back to the wall, making sure Carolina wasn't too far away for her to grab should the need arise.

The half-hour passed quickly, the women speaking good English.

"Carolina, time's up. We need to go."

"I'm not quite finished," Carolina said.

"I can give you five more minutes, and then we're leaving," Mac said firmly. "Understood?" To her relief, Carolina asked her question and after the women answered, she wound things up, standing and thanking them very much for their time and for agreeing to speak with her.

As much as they might dislike her, Carolina Eastern had a way of putting people at ease, if she troubled herself, which made her a natural for interviews.

They hustled Carolina out of the apartment block and arrived back at their base two hours later, the trip taking an hour longer than usual because of a dust storm that obscured the city and made travel difficult. Mac prayed the quiet period lasted through all the interviews.

"I want to arrange the next interview for Friday," Carolina said in her usual no-nonsense tone.

Louie frowned. "That doesn't give us long to do our research."

Although she understood the need for the recon trips and the scrupulous planning, Mac just wanted the interviews completed. All she wanted was to get through them alive. Even now her gut hummed with healthy fear. While it made for good reactions, living with constant adrenaline rushes wasn't good for a person. She'd end up with the jitters, jumping at every slight noise.

At base, they piled out of their vehicle.

"Are you going to the gym?" Simon asked.

Mac hesitated, her gaze going to Louie who was speaking to the drivers. "No, I need to check my emails."

Simon nodded. "Take care." The honest concern in his face and voice brought the prickle of tears to her eyes.

"I will." Mac strode away, heading to her room. She sat on the edge of Louie's bunk to unlace her boots. The tremor of her fingers started then, reaction setting in. Her hands shook so badly she tangled the lace of her right boot into a stubborn knot. A strangled curse squeezed past her tight lips.

The door to their room opened and Louie stepped inside. He took one look and was at her side with two long strides.

"Let me, sweetheart," he said, gently knocking her hands aside. With competent hands, he untangled the knot and slid the boot off her foot.

Mac studied his face through her tear-blurred vision, waiting for his chiding words. They didn't come. Instead he helped her remove her protective vest and then pushed her onto his bunk, sliding in after her. He drew her into his arms and held her.

"It's okay, sweetheart. You did a good job today." He smoothed his hand over her tightly bound hair and pressed her face against his shoulder. His arms surrounded her, the scent of soap, dust and musky sweat familiar and welcoming. Gradually her panic started to recede, and her limbs ceased trembling. Just being with Louie soothed her, his strong arms representing security. Safety. Mac squeezed her eyes closed and realized she'd been fooling herself. This thing between them wasn't anything remotely resembling friends with benefits. She had feelings for him. Somewhere along the line he'd grabbed her heart.

"I DON'T BELIEVE IT," Mac muttered, scanning the contents of her email again.

"Problem?" Louie ambled across the bedroom to stare over her shoulder. Mac didn't even think about hiding the email from him, which rammed home her worry that she'd fallen for him. She valued her independence and had never willingly shared her personal life with a man.

"My father is sneaking from the home again, staking out the vineyard down the road." What the hell did she do? The director's frustration came through clearly in his email. Her father was disrupting the smooth running of the home.

"What are you going to do?"

Mac shrugged. It was all she could manage while trying to keep other emotions at bay—the fear for her father, anger at the disease and a sense of helplessness because she couldn't be there to intervene on her father's behalf.

"I have an idea," Louie said. "I have a friend who lives in Papakura. I was in the SAS with him. Why don't I give him all the details and he can keep an eye on your father?"

"But the director won't let in visitors who aren't family. It's for the patients' safety."

"So tell him Nikolai is your cousin or better yet, that Summer, Nikolai's wife, is your cousin. She's returned to Auckland and wants to visit her uncle."

"But it's a hassle for them. This is my problem to fix. I'll think of something."

"And if you don't? What will you do if they decide your father is too much trouble? You wouldn't want them to confine him."

Confinement would kill her father. Mac dragged a hand through her hair, wincing when she ripped a hair clip free. "I don't know." She removed the clip and jammed it back in place, the faint sting of her scalp bringing home the truth. For once she needed to rely on someone else.

"Do you think your friends would mind checking on my father? And maybe giving him orders each day? I think he forgets." The bloody disease. She hated seeing the decline in her father's mind. Hard enough that he didn't recognize her anymore, but seeing his pride suffer on the brief occasions when he remembered hurt far worse.

"I'll ring Nikolai and ask him," Louie said, his hand squeezing her shoulder.

Warmth swelled inside her. She closed her eyes briefly, fighting the tender emotions. They had no place on the battlefront. "Thank you."

Louie checked his watch. "I'll go and ring him now. If

he's not there, I'll leave a message for him to ring me. Why don't you email the director and tell him your cousin has been in touch? Get Nikolai and Summer Tarei put on the official visitors' list."

"Are you sure your friend won't mind?" She snorted, a trace of amusement in the sound despite her anxiety for her father. "You know the director assured me they could handle my father. I chose this particular home because of their great reputation with Alzheimer patients."

"Your father isn't ordinary. He's a military man. We're different," Louie stated.

Mac liked the fact Louie included her in the group. She was good at her job. After all, her father had shaped her, rearing her like a young soldier. "I don't think the director bargained on a military man."

"Nikolai will do this. I would do anything for Nikolai and Jake, and they'd do the same for me."

Mac understood the sentiment and had seen the same deep friendships with her father and his army mates. The men fought and lived together in close proximity, facing danger and putting their lives in the hands of their fellow soldiers. They suffered through the same experiences, had the same mental traumas, and that bond made them closer than blood relations. Unfortunately, none of her fathers' military friends were around to offer help. "Thanks, Louie.

I appreciate this. I'll email the director now."

"Don't worry, Mac. Everything will turn out okay."

Mac forced a smile, trying not to worry. She wished she shared Louie's confidence.

CHAPTER EIGHT

SIX DAYS LATER

"DID YOU HEAR THAT girl talking on the cell phone again?" Mac asked Carolina when they left the site of the second interview.

"What girl?" Louie demanded.

"There was a girl at the first place," Mac said. "A teenager. We didn't see her, but after we arrived, the phone went a few times. The same thing happened today."

"Don't be stupid." Carolina opened her mouth in a dainty yawn. "There's nothing sinister about a kid and a phone. It was a young girl. Don't you have sisters? Girls are always talking on the phone. Boys too."

"It might be innocent," Louie said. "What does your gut say?"

Mac thought back to the hour-long visit. "I don't know about my gut, but today I felt as if I were in the crosshairs of a rifle the entire time we were there."

"See, this is my problem with the whole deal," Louie said to Carolina. "We can't control who they have inside their house because we can't search it beforehand. We can only secure the perimeter."

"You're paranoid," Carolina said to Mac. "I have one more interview to complete. You can't bail on me now."

"We're not bailing," Mac said before Louie could snarl at Carolina and upset her. "All we're saying is that we want to take things easy and try to control the variables."

"We could send in a team earlier," Tai suggested, flexing the arm where he'd managed to cop a bullet scratch. It didn't seem to slow him down, since the man was always sharp and alert. "Keep the place under surveillance to see if anyone suspicious enters the building before we arrive."

"That's not a bad idea." Louie nailed Carolina with a hard stare. "Send us the information as usual. We want one extra day to prepare this time. This is nonnegotiable."

"We'll see about that," Carolina muttered as they stopped outside her lodgings. She stomped from the vehicle, her displeasure clear in her determined departure.

Tai shook his head. "She's not a good person to cross."

"It can't be helped," Louie said. "I'd rather have her

pissed and alive and the rest of us in one piece. We'll have a strategic meeting when we get back."

They drove to home base without incident, their meeting going well as they formulated a plan of attack and lots of variations in case everything went to hell.

"I'm going to check my email," Mac said.

"No problem." Louie watched her walk away, his gaze lingering on her butt. A sharp nudge in his ribs ripped his attention free. "What the hell..."

Simon scowled. "Do you want everyone to notice?"

"Notice what?" Louie decided to play dumb.

"*Exactly.*"

"Do you have anything to add to our plan?"

"Nah, it's good. Unless Carolina comes back with something off the wall, we should be sweet." Simon paused. "You know we could always turn up an hour earlier or later than we'd planned."

"Not a bad idea. Let's keep that in reserve. I'll be glad when this last interview is over," Louie said. "Coming to the gym?"

"Yeah. See you there," Simon said.

Hopefully not straightaway. He'd hated every moment of the two interviews Carolina Eastern had arranged so far, spending the time strung out and jittery, every sense hyperalert. He'd managed to hide it, but the third one might be the death of him.

Mac was still checking her email when he arrived in their room. She glanced up, her eyes red, her face shiny with tears.

Alarm shot through him. "What's wrong?"

"Nothing." She scrubbed at her face with her hands. "Nothing's wrong. These are happy tears. Your friend's wife, Summer, sent me an email. She said Dad is fine, although insistent that the people at the vineyard are doing something illegal. Your friend is going to investigate." Her eyes shone with gratitude. "My father insists on checking out the place again, and your friend is going with him. That's the best way to handle my father. He's stubborn."

"It's obviously hereditary," Louie said.

Mac didn't bite at his comment. She stood and threw her arms around his neck, pulling his head down so she could kiss him. Louie wasn't about to argue about a little lip lock. The more time he spent with her, the more he was convinced she was the woman he wanted to live with for the rest of his life.

Their lips met, gliding together with the ease of familiarity. Her taste rolled over him, her lithe body pressed close to his. Her soft groan went straight to his groin, his libido going from low simmer to a conflagration at her first touch.

"Mac, sweetheart." Louie pulled away a fraction, dropping his hands to cup her backside to hold her in place. "I need you." His hips moved, rubbing his cock against her stomach in illustration.

She laughed. "You always need me."

"Newsflash, I'm breathing and I'm a guy."

"It wouldn't be as much fun if you were a girl." Her tongue slid over her bottom lip, moistening it while she unfastened the top button of his shirt.

"Your mouth is so sexy. I like kissing it. I enjoy it pressed against my skin."

"Like this?" She skimmed her lips over the skin in the V of his shirt. She lifted her head to nibble at his neck. "Or like that?"

"All of it." Hell, he enjoyed it all. From the first touch, his future was set, and he'd tried to subtly woo her. At least she always welcomed his touch, and she'd started to share her private life with him. That was a start. "I told Simon I'd meet him in the gym."

"We'd better hurry this party along then."

The sparkle in her eyes and the husky note in her voice sent a signal straight to his balls. He stared for an instant, mesmerized by the naughty grin on her face then she went to her knees in front of him. Competent hands unfastened his belt and worked down his zipper.

Anticipation thrummed through him as he stared at her head. She brushed her cheek against his erection, humming lightly. Although he'd planted his feet solidly on the floor, he wondered if he'd manage to stay upright when she put her mouth on him.

"We'll do it this way now," she said, tugging on the waistband of his boxers. His clothing rustled as she yanked his trousers partially down his legs and dragged his boxer waistband down until it rested below his scrotum, lifting his balls and cock higher.

"What about you?"

"I can wait until tonight."

Louie made a sound of approval. "Sounds like a plan." A hell of a good plan.

"I suppose I should hurry."

"Simon is waiting."

She glanced up at him through her dark lashes, her sexy lips pursed. This was the carefree woman he'd met in Fiji. Full of fun and open to experimentation. Her autumn hair alive with color and her golden eyes full of sensual promise. They'd made love outside in the cool night breeze and spent countless pleasurable hours in one of their rooms. "You'll have to tell him something came up." The deliberate drag of her tongue from the base of his cock to the tip sent a surge of pleasure through him.

"I doubt those are details he wants to hear."

"I'm sure you'll come up with something." Her tongue swirled over the head of his shaft then her mouth opened, letting his cock slide inside. The heat of her mouth seared him, made his heart beat faster and his breathing stutter. She took him deeper, sliding the sensitive underside along her tongue.

Louie had to hold on to something, had to anchor himself. He gripped one of her shoulders and slid his other hand into the mass of her hair. She worked his cock, humming, the vibration in her mouth and throat echoing the length of his body. The heat—it fired through him. So good. So bloody good. And the sexy sounds she made, her sighs of approval.

"Mac, I...hell...please let me move." His hips jerked even as he said the words, the need to thrust, to feel more of his cock surrounded by the hot moistness of her mouth. The rest of their surroundings faded away, his narrow focus on Mac and the pleasure she sent reeling through him.

She sucked hard and did something wriggly with her tongue, stroking all the good spots at once. His seed bubbled in his tight balls. Damn, this was good. He wanted to make it last, wanted to do this with her forever.

His woman.

The possessive thoughts flooded his mind, filled his

body as he came, unable to hold back a second longer. "Mac," he whispered hoarsely, the pleasure holding him in its grip, the spasms of his cock seeming to go on for a long time.

She pulled back and grinned up at him. "Worth waiting for?"

"Hell yeah." Louie hauled her to her feet and wrapped her in his arms, kissing her slow and deep with every bit of the possession he felt. He lifted his head, taking pleasure in the dazed expression in her golden-brown eyes, the swollen red lips. He smoothed his thumb over her bottom lip, tempted to rip off his clothes, her clothes and spend the next hour loving her. Only Simon's disapproval stopped him. "I guess I'd better go."

Mac wrinkled her cute, freckled nose. "We don't want Simon thumping on our bedroom door again."

Louie released her with real regret, wanting to kiss each of the freckles that had popped out with the sunshine. He yanked up his pants so he didn't trip and went looking for a T-shirt and some shorts. "Later," he promised, loving the flash of emotion in her eyes, the silent agreement.

Oh yeah. Mac belonged to him and soon, very soon, he'd prove it to her.

THE NEXT MORNING MAC signed in to her email with the usual trepidation. At least she hadn't received an irate phone call from the director. No news was good news.

"Anything from Nikolai or Summer?" Louie asked from the bottom bunk.

She glanced up at him, smiling at the picture he made. His hair stuck up a bit and he had a hickey on his chest to the right of his left nipple. Kind of difficult to explain that to the curious. "I marked you."

"Doesn't matter."

"Don't you mind about gossip?"

"We're not letting this affect our jobs. If anything we're both functioning better than most of the guys. I won't go around showing it like a badge, but I'm not ashamed of it either."

Warmth danced inside Mac as she glanced back at the laptop screen. Ah, she was in. She tapped in her password and waited. "Summer has emailed." Mac clicked on the email and scanned the contents. "Well, hell," she muttered.

"What?"

"Your friend Nikolai and my father have busted a marijuana grower. They had a special shade house and were growing the stuff. The police arrested five people. I don't believe it."

"Your father is sharp," Louie said with a chuckle. "Just

as well we got Nikolai on the job." He glanced at his watch. "Do you want to ring Nikolai later to get the details?"

"I'd like that. I'd like to thank him."

"When we get back from our morning sortie. We're escorting a reporter to the airport and picking up a couple of new recruits."

Mac fired off a quick thank you and mentioned they'd ring later, around nine in the evening New Zealand time. "Aren't you getting out of bed?"

"Nope. Not until I get a morning kiss and cuddle."

Mac stared at Louie, wondering how they'd reached this point of intimacy when she'd intended to keep away from emotional entanglements.

"Mac?"

"I might have a little time before I hit the shower."

"Move your arse then. We need to make good use of your free time."

Mac found herself walking to the bunk and sliding onto the narrow mattress into Louie's arms without an argument. Their lips met in a hungry kiss, as if they hadn't touched each other for weeks. Her womb clenched with need, her tissues swollen and damp. Louie dragged her under him, parted her legs and worked his cock inside her channel before she could blink. He pulled free and slid deep again with a slow stroke. She sighed, melting into him, and enjoying the lazy build of pleasure. It flared hotter and brighter until she exploded, dragging Louie with her. As they came down from the high, Mac wondered how she'd manage when Louie left, and she had to re-up because she had no other option.

THE PLANNING FOR CAROLINA Eastern's third interview took much longer than the others, held up by an increase in military action in the area they wanted to visit. Now, a month later, they were finally on their way to the small village outside the city.

Heat shimmered on the road in twisting and glistening patterns. Sweat coated Louie's body beneath the protective vest. The sky was a vivid blue with not a cloud in sight.

A helicopter passed overhead, and over to his right, a plane circled, ready to land at the airport. Three-quarters of an hour into the journey to the village everything had gone to plan, and they hadn't come across anything unusual, not even a roadblock.

"All quiet." Simon's voice crackled through the radio.

Carolina Eastern snorted, her dark brows drawing together. "What does he expect? You've both behaved like old women with this trip."

"Better old women than dead," Garrett snapped.

Louie sent Garrett a warning glance even though he appreciated the sentiment. Carolina was frustrated. Hell, they were all edgy after the on-off nature of this last interview.

Ahead, a burst of gunfire shattered the peace. It sounded close. Too close.

"I don't freaking believe it," Carolina spat. "Please tell me we're not returning."

"Do you practice being a bitch or does it come natural?" Mac asked.

There was a startled silence before Carolina laughed. "I guess it comes naturally. Sorry. I'm aggravated with the holdups. I don't mean to take it out on all of you."

"I'd never have guessed," Mac said, lifting her chin in defiance.

Louie bit his inner lip, trying not to laugh at the two women. Garrett didn't even try. He chuckled out loud.

"Should I keep going?" the driver asked, slowing when another volley of fire sounded to their right.

"Yeah, keep going." Louie hoped he was doing the right thing.

Their driver continued, the gunfire gradually receding. They all relaxed a fraction, eyes scanning the road on both sides as they continued their journey. Gradually, the road opened up, and they saw fewer military vehicles, although overhead the *whop-whop* of helicopters continued. Sometimes they drew return fire, spurts of *rat-tat-tats* echoing around them. Smoke filled the air and flames licked at a building. No one bothered to try to put out the fire.

They traveled down a rutted road. In some parts, it seemed as if they drove through a junkyard, the skeletons of discarded vehicles littering the sides of the road.

"Almost there," Carolina said.

"When are you heading home to the States?" Mac asked.

"Next month. I'm looking forward to the break, but I'll probably be bored in a week."

"Not me," Louie said firmly. "It will be good to walk down a street and not worry about being shot at."

The village consisted of ten whitewashed buildings. To their right a young kid herded a motley assortment of goats to grazing. A couple of young boys played with a ball, kicking it around outside one of the buildings, the sight of them reassuring Louie. They laughed and waved as soon as they saw them driving past.

"Looking good," he radioed Simon in the other vehicle. "How does it look where you are?" As they'd discussed earlier, Simon's vehicle had arrived early and parked out of sight to watch. Despite the radio report from Simon, he still carefully scanned the surroundings, as did the others in his vehicle. When nothing out of the ordinary occurred, the driver pulled up in front of the house Carolina wanted to visit.

"Hustle," Louie said to Carolina. "I want you inside quickly and out of the open."

Mac climbed out, waited for Carolina to exit and fall into step with her. Garrett flanked her on the other side, and they moved at a brisk pace.

The back of Louie's neck started to prickle. Every instinct told him someone watched them. Cursing softly, he scanned their surroundings. He couldn't see anything unusual. "Neck's prickling. Anyone see trouble?"

"Nothing, boss."

"I can't see anything." Mac stopped abruptly. "Man at ten o'clock. Down. *Get down*." She shoved Carolina, pushing her down onto the hard ground. Carolina screamed. Shots fired, seeming to come from all directions.

"Back to the vehicles," Louie shouted. "Pull out. Pull out now!"

Shots came faster, kicking up dust. Close. Too close. No way to make it back to the vehicle. Mac grabbed Carolina by the back of her flak jacket, hauled her to her feet. Garrett ran on Carolina's other side, pausing to fire cover shots while they retreated. Leaving Garrett behind, Mac dragged Carolina to the nearest dwelling and shoved her inside, heart pumping when bullets flicked up from the ground as she ran.

"Keep down. Don't give them a target," Louie hollered when Carolina struggled to regain her feet.

With their VIP safe, Mac's attention went to the rest of her team. Louie let off a volley of shots and raced across the open ground to reach cover. With the return fire slowing, Mac took the time to scan the vicinity. She caught a flicker of movement in her peripheral vision. A kid. She relaxed until she saw the gun aimed at Garrett.

"Watch it!" Mac fired, hoping like hell that Garrett made it to safety.

"Oomph!" Garrett leaped for the doorway, landing hard. Louie hauled him inside. Their driver was a few steps behind.

"Check the building. Make sure it's empty," Louie ordered.

"I'm on it," Mac said, scuttling past a window before rising to race up the flight of stairs to the next floor. A sound made her freeze. Extending her weapon, she slid closer to the room to her right. When she didn't hear another sound, she peered around the corner. A flash of movement had her pulling the trigger even as her mind registered it was a group of women and children. Somehow Mac managed to pull her weapon up, sending the bullets high into the wall.

Her weapon fell silent. Heart pumping with adrenaline, she scanned the room. The four women of various ages sat huddled in the corner, along with two toddlers. Their faces held terror, yet they scarcely made a sound.

Mac lowered her weapon, tried to control her trembling. "It's okay," she croaked.

Thumping footsteps heralded an imminent arrival.

"Mac?" Garrett hollered.

One of the toddlers started crying. Mac didn't blame him.

"Don't shoot! It's women and children."

Garrett thundered to a halt behind her and the second toddler howled.

"You're scaring them."

"Weapons check?"

Mac doubted they would cause trouble. "Just about to do it."

"I'll check the other rooms," Garrett said, slipping away before she could answer.

One of the local women let out a horrified sound and leapt to her feet. "Babee!"

"Garrett, I think there's a kid in one of the other rooms."

Mac cut the woman off and briskly patted her down.

"All clear," Garrett said, returning with a baby. He handed it over to the woman, scanned the room briskly and went to look out the window at the renewed gunfire. "Shit, looks as if we'll have to hunker down. Insurgents are everywhere."

An RPG hit in front of the building. The *rat-a-tat* of gunfire following, along with loud shouting.

"Bastards are shooting out our tires," Garrett said.

"Any other exits?"

"Nah, just the door we came in and the windows along the front."

Mac swiftly checked the rest of the women for weapons and found none. "I'll go and check with Louie." She hurried down the stairs.

"We heard gunfire," Louie said.

"It was me. I almost shot the group of women up there," she shouted over a wave of incoming fire. "Where's Simon?"

"I don't know. Radio's out."

Mac shared a glance with Louie. "Looks as if we're on our own."

Carolina stood.

"What the hell are you doing?" Mac snarled, grabbing her, forcing her back down with brute strength. Stupid bitch. She'd get herself killed if she wasn't careful.

Carolina struggled, eyes flashing with dislike. "I want to join the other women."

Mac glanced at Louie, and he nodded. "Less to worry about," he said.

Another barrage of fire claimed his attention.

"Let's go," Mac said to Carolina. "Keep your head low until we can't be seen through the windows."

"Wait. Let me get my bag." Carolina grabbed it, gave a crisp nod and scurried toward the stairs, following orders for once.

"Stay with the other women. Don't move from here," Mac ordered once they reached the room with Garrett and the women.

"I'll do my interview," Carolina said.

Speechless, Mac merely nodded and went to join Garrett. Outside, a crowd gathered. Bodies strewed the ground in front of the dwelling. Several men were shooting round after round into their empty vehicle.

Mac bit her bottom lip, trying to control the dart of fear swirling inside her. Trapped. And the shooters didn't seem to care if they died or not. She peered out the window as another wave of fire came, the insurgents shooting over their fallen comrades.

A grenade hit the ground in front of the building

and rolled closer, exploding. Constant noise, shouts and gunfire made her head ring. Mac thought about her father and prayed harder as she kept firing shots through the window. She thought about Louie. Damn, she didn't want to die like this.

Her stomach curdled, nausea making her swallow compulsively. A bullet struck the wall not far from her position. A child cried. She heard Carolina's low voice. Unable to hear what she was saying, Mac could guess. She didn't like the other woman much even though she admired her dogged perseverance.

The light was fading, the return fire sporadic.

"You guys okay up there?" Louie called.

"Going strong," Garrett answered for them.

"Casualties?"

"We're good," Mac shouted. "Any word of Simon?"

"Communication is still down."

Outside shouts renewed. The increased noise suggested new recruits had arrived. The laughter and masculine shrieks made Mac think of a night at the pub. Were they high? She'd heard some insurgents pumped themselves full of drugs before a battle. A shiver worked through her, and she wanted to see Louie so bad she almost obeyed the instinct to go to him.

"You okay?" Garrett asked. "Not turning wussy on me?"

"Hell no," Mac replied, but she had to force a grin. Keep talking, she thought. Concentrate on talking and returning fire. It beat worrying about capture. Torture.

"Mac?"

"Yeah?"

"We're not gonna let them into the building," Garrett said in a low voice. "Not gonna happen. Surrender isn't an option here."

She nodded and returned her attention to the road outside.

A shot fired and Garrett went down.

"Man down," Mac shouted.

"I'll take care of him," Carolina said in a firm voice. She slid across the floor to Garrett. "You okay?"

"Yeah." Garrett peeled his fingers away from his biceps.

"Good," Carolina said crisply. "Get up you lazy bastard and do some work."

Mac gaped in disbelief.

Garrett spluttered then shook his head and chuckled. "Yes, ma'am."

"You guys okay up there?" Louie hollered.

"Yeah," Garrett answered.

The insurgents attacked again, the hail of gunfire making Mac's ears ring. A bullet hit the window frame, sending a fragment of wood into her cheek. Hurt like the devil. She cursed, continued firing. The bodies piled up but still they kept coming. Mac tried not to think of her fellow humans behind the guns, just concentrated on the job at hand, keeping themselves alive and the women with them.

Wave after wave of incoming fire kept them pinned at the windows. Mac pointed her weapon, identified her target, and fired. On automatic. They couldn't afford to let the insurgents get any closer, couldn't let them inside otherwise they'd die. She thought of Louie, worried about his safety. Missed a target. He kept coming, kept coming with a devilish high-pitched shriek. Then he fell. Still.

Concentrate. Focus.

Mac picked off two more men. Another man fired a grenade. It exploded, the flare of light searing on her retinas. Her head rang and the building seemed to tremble. They couldn't hold them off much longer. Damn, she didn't wanna die. She wanted to tell Louie she cared, that their sessions weren't just about burning off the buzz. There was more. But fear had held her back. Now she might not get the chance.

More men. More shots. So tired. They'd run out of ammo soon. Then it would be all over. Mac didn't know if she could take her own life. Preferable to the alternative. Torture. Possible rape. Death.

Then a foreign sound intruded. Garrett whooped. It took Mac longer to recognize the distinct sound of heavy armor. The flare of an explosion lit the buildings, turning them into silhouettes before darkness fell again.

"Simon must have come through," Garrett shouted.

Smoke filled the air. Mac sneezed.

The bark of an AK-47 rent the air. Mac ducked back, another sting in her cheek making her gasp. A wet trickle followed. She dashed away the blood, investigating the spot with her fingertips. A stone fragment. Nothing serious.

Beside her Garrett started cursing. "A fuckin' tooth. Bastard." He fired several shots before gingerly checking his mouth.

"Ouch, that's gonna be expensive," Mac said.

"Tell me about it," Garrett groused, spitting out a mouthful of blood. Something pinged against the wooden floor.

"Yep, that's a tooth all right."

"Hell," Garrett muttered.

Gradually the return fire slowed. The armored vehicle shot off rounds. Garrett and Mac continued to watch, scanning for movement below. The men lying on the ground in front of the building weren't necessarily dead.

"You guys okay up there?" Louie hollered.

"Yeah," Garrett answered.

Exhaustion crept over Mac then as she studied the dark street. The women were quiet, the children asleep. Not even Carolina spoke. The shots died away and everything went eerily quiet.

One of the two armored vehicles stopped outside, and someone climbed out.

"You can come out now," Simon shouted. "Cavalry's here."

"See anything suspicious from up there?" Louie asked from the doorway. His face was gray with dust, but his smile was wide and encouraging.

Mac wanted to set down her weapon and throw herself into his arms, reassure herself he was okay, that she was alive. She forced herself to remain at the window, turned back to scan the street.

"Can't see anything," Garrett said. "Mac?"

"It looks quiet down there. They've retreated." Mac scanned Louie's face. She couldn't wait to get back to their room. Her entire body buzzed like a live wire. She fidgeted, unable to keep still.

Louie winked at her when Garrett wasn't looking. Her heart soared, and she had to bite her bottom lip to halt the crazy urge to tell him she loved him.

"Time to go home, troops," Louie said. "Carolina, I'll

go first then Garrett. You follow Garrett and Mac and the driver will bring up the rear. You will run. You will follow orders."

"Sure," Carolina said agreeably.

Mac shook her head. She'd never understand the other woman.

Carolina spoke to the local woman, said her goodbyes, and followed Louie down the stairs. Mac followed Garrett.

Louie cautiously opened the door and peered outside. "Right. The vehicle is here to take us back. Carolina, you ready?"

She nodded and slid into position behind Garrett. Mac moved in her rear. They ran. Halfway between the dwelling and the vehicle, the hairs at the back of Mac's neck rose. She paused. A flicker of movement caught her attention, and she was moving before the conscious thought formed. A series of shots rang out as Mac shoved Carolina. The reporter screamed as she hit the ground. Time slowed. Fire seared Mac's shoulder and she fell. The hard jolt with the ground crashed time back into place. It felt as if someone had taken to her with a hammer. Shots rang in her ears. Smoke from discharged weapons shrouded her sight. She groaned, struggling to rise.

"Man down! Man down!"

Damn, her shoulder hurt.

Warm liquid seeped down her arm, inside her body armor. She prodded it with her fingers and moaned at the flash of pain. Her fingers came away covered in red.

Blood.

Pain clawed her arm, her shoulder. Her vision wavered, turning to black then nothing registered.

Louie rolled, fear rippling through him when he saw Mac fall. Instinct and training had him returning fire. Chaos reigned, his men shooting on the run. Shots seemed confined to one area. Probably one man. Garrett was already moving, scooping up Mac and shoving her into the rear seat with Carolina. Louie wanted to rip Garrett away and check on Mac himself. He took half a step before his brain kicked into gear. Garrett was their medic, the best person to look after Mac.

"Simon? Status?" he hollered.

Another shot fired and Simon went down. Fuck it! "Man down!"

A single shot went off, kicking up dust at his feet. Grabbing Simon, he backed toward the vehicle, ready to return fire. It wasn't necessary. He jerked the door open and slid inside even as the local driver backed up. One look at Simon's head told him the worst. He wanted to howl. Tears burned his eyes as he checked for a pulse. Nothing. He wrapped his arms around Simon and held his friend,

174

wondering how the hell he'd tell Simon's wife.

"How is she?" Louie asked hoarsely, surprised the words made it past the lump in his throat.

"Damn bullet went in the side of the vest. Shoulder injury. She's tough. She'll make it, if I can stop this goddamn bleeding." Garrett rifled through a bag and opened a sterile pad. "It was a bloody fluke." He situated the pad on the wound. "Carolina, press down on this."

Carolina followed Garrett's order without a murmur.

"Let me look at Simon," Garrett said.

"It's too late. He's gone." A tear ran down Louie's cheek. He wanted to rip things apart, knock heads together. He did neither, instead clamping down on his worry for Mac and retreating to what he knew best. Being a soldier. He gently pushed Simon into the seat beside him, scanned their surroundings, alert for trouble, and did his job.

"How is she?" Louie had lost count of the number of times he'd asked. One thing he knew for sure was that he loved her and if he couldn't talk to her soon, he'd go crazy.

"She's awake. You can go in," Garrett said.

Louie strode into the dimmed room. "Mac?"

"Louie?"

"Yeah, sweetheart. It's me. How do you feel?" He leaned over and pressed a gentle kiss to her lips. To hell with protocol and what anyone thought.

"Like crap. They're sending me to Germany and probably home to New Zealand after that."

"It takes a while to recuperate from a shoulder injury," he said, his gut sinking at the news. Garrett had told him they'd managed to extract the bullet, although he was worried about the damage to Mac's shoulder. "It makes sense since you only have a couple of months left of your contract."

"But I need to work. I can't afford not to work."

The lone tear that trickled down her face about killed him. He smoothed it away with his forefinger, swallowing his reluctance at this forced parting. He'd known it would happen sooner or later. It was the nature of their job, but he'd thought he'd have more time to convince her they belonged together. "You can't work until you've healed. Get better. Go home and spend some time with your father."

"At least I'm alive. How is Simon's wife? Did you talk to her?"

"Yeah, I talked to her. She's not doing too good. Went into early labor. She's okay. Had a boy." Louie had to smile. "Simon wanted a girl."

"Wish I could have made the service. I liked Simon. He was a good man." Mac sniffed and wiped the back of her hand under her nose. "Damn, I hate feeling weak. I know you're right. I'll go home, get better and sign up again in a few months."

Not if he had his way. "That's the best thing, sweetheart. I'll come to see you again before you leave. Take care." He wanted to tell her he loved her, wanted to tell her so bad. Instead he confined himself to another kiss, a caress of her cheek. He took a last lingering look and walked away.

Chapter Nine

Two and a half months later, New Zealand

Mac picked up her father from the home for the day and drove to Papakura. Summer had rung, invited her to visit for the day and told her to bring her father. When Mac protested, Summer had overridden her objections and said Mac's father had visited them a few times and he wasn't a problem. He liked gardening and had been a big help.

Mac yawned, tensing her jaw as she glanced at her father who was waving at the kid in the car in front. At least he seemed happy. She wasn't sleeping and knew she'd lost weight. The constant flashbacks to the day she was injured, and Simon died didn't help. She knew she should start training to regain her fitness and sign up for another term in Iraq. So far, other things had come up and she hadn't followed through and contacted Chesterton UK's head office.

Mac snorted, and flicked on her indicator, pulling out to the fast lane of the motorway. That wasn't the truth. She was waiting to see Louie. She had to return, but she'd like to spend a week or two with Louie before she traveled back to Baghdad. Maybe he didn't want to see her. He hadn't phoned, hadn't even emailed.

She'd emailed him. Once. A brief email to say she'd arrived home.

Mac took the Karaka exit and turned right toward Bottle Top Bay where Nikolai and Summer Tarei lived.

"How is security at the home now?" she asked her father. He'd looked older but happy, which pleased her. And while he hadn't known her name, he recognized her sometimes. The director said that since the drug bust by the police he seemed more settled. He'd also mentioned that her father enjoyed the day visits and trips to visit his niece. She didn't know how to start saying thank you to Nikolai and Summer. She was hoping the gift basket of handmade soaps and lotions would be a step in the right direction.

"Good," her father said.

"Do you like it?"

"The kid is waving at me."

"She is," Mac said, smiling. It was hard not being able to have a conversation with her father. It broke her heart, but it didn't stop her from trying.

Mac followed the signposts for Bottle Top Bay and drove slowly past the line of houses until she reached the white one with a bed of red pansies growing in front.

"This is our stop, Dad." She pulled up beside a black SUV and switched off the ignition. Mac helped her father out, grabbed her handbag and the gift basket, and herded him up the path to the front door.

The door opened before they arrived, a very pregnant woman grinning at them and waving at her father. "Hi, Jack," she said, kissing his cheek. "In you go. You remember the way?"

Mac watched in awe. Summer was great with him. She swallowed, aware of the tinge of jealousy flickering through her.

"You must be Mac," Summer said. "I've been looking forward to meeting you. Come inside. The others are out the back in the garden."

"Others?" She handed Summer the gift basket. "This is a thank-you gift."

"Ooh, you didn't have to, but I adore presents. Nikolai will tell you. My Uncle Henry and his wife Veronica have popped over and a couple of Nikolai's army buddies. It's just family." She ushered Mac inside and through the house.

Her father was already sitting down under the shade of an umbrella talking to an older couple. His laugh rang out and tears stung her eyes. She scanned the rest of the faces, gasping when she came to Louie.

"Louie," she whispered. She took two steps and came to an uncertain halt. Embarrassment flooded her cheeks. What if he didn't—?

"Mac." He crossed the distance separating them with giant strides, wrapped his arms around her and kissed her, despite the audience.

Her fingers gripped his shoulders, and she kissed him back, putting everything she felt, all her confusion into the kiss. She'd missed him so much, thought of a thousand things throughout the day to tell him. Then she'd told herself they'd merely been friends who were there for each other, the loving a release of tension. A way of surviving their crazy world.

Louie pulled back a fraction, pressing his forehead against hers before saying, "Let's go inside for a bit of privacy."

It was only then that she became aware of the hoots and whistles, the teasing coming from his friends.

Louie took her hand and led her inside. "Don't mind them." He tugged her close again and smiled down into her eyes. "God, I've missed you. How are you? Summer said you're healed now."

"Why didn't you call? Email me?" Mac blurted. It wasn't what she meant to say, and she bit her bottom lip in consternation.

"Because I didn't want to pressure you. I wanted you to realize you missed me without pushing. I didn't want to force myself on you. You are glad to see me?" His brown gaze drilled into her, demanding answers, the pressure of his fingers on her upper arms telling her how much investment he had in her answer.

"I'm glad to see you." Mac buried her hands in his dark hair and brushed a kiss across his jaw. "I missed you," she whispered, closing her eyes. "I didn't expect to miss you so much."

"Good." Louie took possession of her mouth again, the kiss demanding and hungry and she returned it with reckless abandon. She hadn't realized how much she'd come to rely on having him around as a sounding board, a friend. A lover. Pleasure roared through her at his touch, his large callused hand gripping her bottom and lifting her against him. His cock was a hard wedge between them, and a soft moan emerged when he guided her against him, the rub of her clit bringing a surge of sweet anticipation.

"Louie, put her down," Summer said from behind them. "You can't do that here."

"Why not?" Louie let her slide down his body and Mac had to suppress her moan of pleasure.

Finally, her feet touched the ground again, embarrassment at her abandon having her gaze shifting to her feet.

"It's only Summer," he whispered, tucking a lock of hair behind her ear. "You're going to have to turn around and face her some time. Come on." Taking her hand in his, he led her back outside.

A tall, dark-haired man with a slight limp came forward, his hand extended. "Since Louie's manners have disappeared—I'm Nikolai, Summer's husband." He indicated the older couple. "This is Henry and Veronica, our neighbors, and this is Jake. Louie, you can let the girl go."

"I don't want to." Louie wrapped his arm around her shoulders. "Besides, I'm not letting Jake near her."

Summer winked at her husband. "We could have some fun with this. Louie and Jake gave Nikolai and me a really hard time when we first met. You'll have to forgive us, but we're having fun teasing Louie."

"Would you like a drink, Mac?" Jake asked, taking her

arm, and tugging her away from Louie. "You can tell me all about yourself while we're getting the drinks."

Everyone laughed at Louie's low growl, even her father. Mac let Jake lead her inside to the kitchen, the dark-haired man flirting the entire time.

"Are you sure you wouldn't rather go out with me?" Jake asked, grinning at her as he poured a juice for Summer. "Wine, beer or a juice for you?"

"I'll take a juice please."

"Will your father have a beer?"

"A beer is fine."

"I hear you took a bullet in Iraq."

Mac scowled. "Damn thing got through my flak jacket. Made a mess of my shoulder. It was a real fluke."

"It happens that way sometimes," Jake said, handing her a beer and a glass of orange juice. "You've recovered okay?"

"Yeah, I have full motion in the shoulder again." Mac didn't want to talk about her return to Iraq. "Are you still on active duty?"

"Yeah. Come on. Louie's probably stewed enough. I don't suppose you'd consider putting on some lipstick and kissing me?"

Mac snorted on seeing the devilment in his eyes. "That would go down well."

"I know. So can we do it?"

"No." Mac was still smiling when she walked outside to join the others. Her gaze connected with Louie's and the air bled from her lungs. A tiny shiver of awareness swept her body, settling between her thighs. She swallowed, curling her fingers into her palms to still the impulse to walk up to him and run her fingers over his broad chest, lean into his muscular body and rub against him in blatant invitation. Instead, she flashed him a smile and delivered the beer to her father.

Louie couldn't take his eyes off Mac. Her loose hair fell around her shoulders, the autumn colors bright and alive in the sunshine. She wore a yellow top and a pair of jeans that showcased her figure, hugging her hips and bottom. He wondered if his hand would burn when he touched her hair. His lips quirked upward at the fanciful thought.

The faint shadows beneath her eyes worried him more. And her smile. He knew her well enough to see she forced it at times. The others wouldn't notice but he had. He'd missed her so bloody much, the time after she'd left Iraq was sheer torture. Until her departure, he hadn't realized how she'd kept him grounded while doing a difficult job. It wasn't just the sex. He'd missed talking with her about their missions, sharing a joke and having someone to hold during the hours when sleep wouldn't come. And Simon. No one would understand his loss quite like Mac.

Right now, all he wanted to do was drag Mac away to a quiet place where they could get horizontal, where he could touch her and reassure himself she wasn't a desert mirage. They'd both made it out of Iraq in one piece. He glanced at his mates and found them watching him. Nikolai and Jake, curse their hides, knew exactly what was on his mind.

"We're having a barbeque tonight," Nikolai said. "Why don't you stay?"

"Thanks, but I have to get Dad back to the home," Mac said.

Jake winked at Nikolai. "Summer won't mind if you stay the night. There's plenty of room."

"Feel free to offer my house," Nikolai said with a chuckle.

Jake shrugged. "I knew you wouldn't mind."

Finally, tired of the sly digs, Louie spoke out. "Mac and I are going out tonight."

"We are?" Her initial confusion transformed into enlightenment. Her eyes rounded. She glanced at her father then back at him before nodding.

Louie's breath eased from him, along with tension. At least she was willing to talk. He hoped she'd be willing to listen. Compromise. Hell, who was he trying to kid? Without Mac, his life wasn't the same. His dream of retiring to a beach didn't seem important. If Mac insisted on re-upping, then he would too.

"Mac, your father can stay with us tonight," Summer said. When she had trouble sitting, Nikolai helped her, the gentle look of awe on his face when he placed his hand on Summer's stomach feeling too private for Louie to watch.

He glanced away to catch Jake's grin. His friend intended to give him a hard time. Louie didn't care, although he'd take the opportunity to tell Jake about payback being a bitch. With Nikolai, he'd put up with whatever his friend dished out because he reckoned he deserved it.

Two hours tops and they were out of here. He loved spending time with his friends, but he wanted Mac more.

He made it to the hour-and-a-half mark by not looking at Mac. His dick was hard and anyone with half a brain would know it. No one could ever accuse his friends of being thick.

"Mac, we're leaving," he said, taking three steps to reach her side. He grabbed her hand and tugged.

"We haven't had a chance to get to know Mac," Jake protested with a flash of white teeth.

"And you're not going to," Louie snapped. "We're leaving. Do you need to say goodbye to your father?"

"But what about the home? I have to ring them."

"I'll take care of that for you," Summer said. "I'll walk you out and do it now."

"You don't have to go now," Nikolai seconded Jake.

"Yes, we do," Louie snarled, ready to hit them both. He pressed her against his side and wrapped his arm around her waist. His possessive manner didn't go unnoticed, his mates and Summer all smirking at him. Louie didn't care. He pressed his face into her hair and inhaled the scent of a flowery shampoo. "Are you ready to leave?"

Mac nodded, the expression in her eyes sinking straight to his cock. Lord, he thought he'd die if he didn't get inside her soon. Louie hurried her outside to his vehicle, opening the door for her.

"What about my car?"

"Leave it here. We'll collect it tomorrow." Louie climbed behind the wheel and backed out.

"Where are we going?"

"My place."

"I didn't know you had a house."

"Rental," he said, reached over to grasp her hand. He needed the contact.

It was the fastest trip he'd ever made from Nikolai's place to his rental on the other side of Papakura. He parked in his driveway and climbed out.

"Inside," he ordered. Part of him was surprised when she

didn't argue about his high-handed manner. He unlocked his front door and stood aside while she entered, forcing himself not to touch her until they were inside.

He closed the door with a soft click and turned to her, all bets off now. He intended to touch to his heart's content.

"I've missed you, sweetheart." Louie closed the distance between them, caging Mac against the wall with his hands on either side of her head. He breathed in her scent, wallowing in it. He smelled her shampoo again and the faint fragrance of soap. She'd lost weight and looked tired. Worried even, and he hated to think he'd add to her stress, but it was a conversation they had to have if they intended to stay together.

But first...

"Stop staring," she complained, wrinkling her nose.

"But you're so pretty."

"I have scars."

"Battle wounds, sweetheart. It's the nature of the job. You're alive and that's all that matters." A shudder raced through him at the thought of how close she'd come to death. And she thought he worried about a few stupid scars. "Do you know what I'm going to do now?"

"Kiss me?"

"I'm going to strip off all your clothes and explore your body. I intend to make love to you until you feel so much pleasure you'll scream." He enjoyed seeing her eyes widen and the faint color creep into her cheeks. "And then I'm going to do it all over again. We'll start right now."

Before she could say a word, he dipped his head and took her mouth. It was a dominant kiss, confident and demanding. He nipped her bottom lip, soothed it with the lave of his lips and swept his tongue inside to taste her. The feel of her, so familiar and full of memories, burst over him, her eager response fueling his need.

Louie pressed closer, savoring the brush of her breasts, the hard nipples poking into his chest. The grip of her fingers on his shoulders. One of her hands moved down his back and came to rest on his butt, dragging him closer, telling him without words that this thing between them wasn't one-way.

Mac tore her mouth from his. "Clothes. Off. Now." She pushed him away and yanked at his top button. It came undone after a quick struggle. Louie almost laughed as she started on the second button, the trembling hands telling him exactly what he wanted to know. She was desperate too. It gave him hope.

With a whoop, he lifted Mac, swinging her into his arms. He hurried down the passage to his bedroom and dropped her on his bed. Louie took a moment to enjoy the sight. Her eyes sparkled with sexual excitement as she unfastened the two buttons on her yellow knit top. She whipped it over her head and disposed of her bra. A slow grin built as he watched her wriggle out of her jeans and curse when she realized she still wore her footwear. Stepping forward, he unbuckled the sandals and pulled off her jeans and underwear. Grinning, Mac settled back on his bed and pinched her nipple.

"Trying to get my attention?"

"Is it working?" she asked, her voice slightly breathless.

Louie cupped his erection, his brows rising. "What do you think?"

"That maybe you need more incentive to hurry." She parted her legs, flashing pink lady parts at him.

He swallowed at the sheen of moisture and sank onto the bed. "I need to taste." Cupping her butt with his hands, he lifted her to his mouth. Starting out slowly, he blew a stream of moist air.

"More," she demanded in a breathy voice.

"How's this?" He massaged her clit with a firm stroke then backed off, circling the hard nub with his tongue.

"Better," she said with a sigh. "Much better."

Louie lapped at the juices spilling from her, loving the moans and the increasingly frantic jerks of her hips. His cock pressed against his fly, the sensation almost painful, but he didn't want to take the time to undress.

Mac wriggled beneath him, and he gripped her hip, holding her still while he took his sweet time tasting her, teasing her.

"Louie," she wailed.

"Play with your breasts again for me. Show me what you like." She didn't hesitate and cupped her right breast before pinching her nipple between finger and thumb.

"Tell me how it feels," he ordered, and flicked her nub with the tip of his tongue. "Tell me."

"My breasts feel heavy. Swollen because I've been thinking about sex."

"Sex with me," Louie said, wanting to make sure and needing her to admit she'd thought about him.

"I've been thinking about you fucking me, the way it feels when you fill me with slow strokes. A vibrator is not the same."

"You used a vibrator?"

Mac glared at him. "Don't sound so offended. Would you rather I'd gone out and found another man?"

Louie didn't even need to think about that. "Hell no."

"So, what do you do when you're frustrated? Did you go out and find a woman?"

"I didn't want another woman. I'm smart enough to know the only woman I want in my bed is you." His words rang between them, stark and full of truth.

"Good answer, soldier," Mac said finally. "Please take off your clothes and put your cock inside me. I'm tired of feeling empty."

Louie leapt off the bed and stripped. He returned to her side and lay back on the bed. "Ride me," he said. "You take what you want." His gaze swept across her face and this time he allowed himself to look at the bullet wound on the left side of her upper body. The wound had healed, the scar still a bright pink against the tan of her skin.

"Ugly, huh?"

"It will fade." Louie pointed to a scar on his right hip. "Caught a piece of metal thrown from a car bomb. Are you going to walk because it's ugly?"

"Of course not."

"Then why would I worry about your scar? You're alive. You're mobile. That's all that's important to me." Louie grasped his cock and pumped it slowly with his hand. Need clawed at him, a bead of pre-cum glistening on the crown of his shaft. He caught Mac watching, the easy glide of her tongue across her bottom lip like a zap to his balls. "Are you just going to watch?"

"You put on a good show."

Louie snorted a laugh. "You like making me suffer."

"No, I don't." Mac straddled his legs and batted his hands away from his cock. "Hands under your head. I want to play."

"I thought you were in a hurry."

"I've changed my mind."

"Just my luck," he muttered.

"Shush or I'll gag you and tie you up. And I don't do wussy girl knots either. If I tie you up, you won't get free until I say so."

Louie stilled. "That's hot."

Mac laughed and grinned at him. "I can probably think up something worse."

"If it involves you and me naked and a horizontal surface, then I'm good."

Mac shook her head and took his cock into her mouth. The swipe of her tongue over the crown and under, followed by a hard suck brought a groan. Mac lifted her head, releasing his shaft with a loud pop.

"Mac," he protested.

"Patience, soldier." She wriggled up a bit, rose above his cock and guided him to her entrance and sank down, taking his cock inside her snug channel.

The tight squeeze of her pussy almost did him in. Willpower. He didn't have any. An electric current surged from his balls, and he mentally stripped his rifle, cleaned each piece and slowly assembled it again. Louie let out a long pent-up breath until she started to move, rocking against him, rising and falling. Her breasts bounced as her movements became more frantic. It was the sexiest thing he'd ever seen. Raw need sprang to life again, and Louie knew he'd never last.

"Mac, I can't hold back."

"No problem." Her gamine grin made his heart stutter, his pulse pound, and his cock swell. He gritted his teeth as she lifted and slid back down. She threw back her head, closing her eyes as she rose and pushed back down, impaling herself. Mac started touching herself, and he watched, entranced at her open pleasure.

The spicy tang of sex filled the air, fire flickering through his body as the need grew in him. He refused to let go, wanting this moment to last as long as possible. But her silken sheath rippled, squeezing his cock.

"This feels good, better than my memory," Mac said. "Much better."

Louie reached up to cup one breast, savoring the warmth of the creamy curve. He pinched her nipple and Mac moaned loudly. "That's new. I like it."

"What? My appreciation?"

"The sounds. I like knowing I can give you pleasure, sweetheart. The sounds you make when you come are hot."

"You make me feel *very* good." Mac slid her finger across

her clit and threw back her head, her body straining toward the pleasure. He felt the surge of wetness and the tight, rhythmic squeeze of her pussy. "Louie," she cried out.

It was a signal for him to let go. His hips jerked and raw, hot pleasure spilled through him. His cock jerked, the spurt of seed splashing into her body. He groaned, the enjoyable spasms continuing for long moments.

Mac fell forward and he wrapped his arms around her, seizing her lips in a hard kiss.

"Mine," he growled against his lips.

"Yours," she agreed without hesitation.

Louie laughed. "I thought you might grab your gun and shoot me."

"You belong to me," she said. "Are you going to shoot me for saying it?"

"Hell no." His cock started to swell again, and he rolled her under him, feasting on her mouth, dragging more of those breathy moans from her as he rocked into her. Her hands laced behind his neck, a rough growl vibrating in his chest when she sucked on his neck. He knew it would leave a mark. Nikolai and Jake would give him a hard time about it and he didn't care. He had Mac in his arms and that's exactly what he wanted.

Cupping her bottom, he lifted her and stroked hard and fast. The feel of her hot walls clamping down on him sent him soaring and he came in a quick burst of pleasure. Knowing she hadn't come again, he pulled out and used his mouth, sucking gently on her clit, stroking and tonguing it until she cried out, shuddering, her eyes dark with ecstasy.

Louie pulled back the covers and crawled under them with Mac, not willing to let her go. They were quiet for a while, but Louie sensed she wasn't sleeping.

"How are you?" he asked. "Really."

"I'm ready to go back to work, but I've been putting it off." Mac pulled away from him a fraction, and he let her so he could see her face.

"Are you scared?" He couldn't imagine having this conversation with any of his other mates.

"No, it's not that." Mac refused to look at him. A good sign? Maybe. Maybe not.

"What then?"

"My head isn't in the job. I know I have to go because I need the money, but you won't be there," she ended in a rush. "You're not going back, are you?"

"If you sign up for another term, I'm heading back to Iraq too." This wasn't the time to play games. "I'm not letting you walk away from me again, Mac."

Mac frowned at him. "You don't want to go back."

"No."

"But you'd go because of me?"

"There's another option, Mac. One you haven't considered." Louie paused, watching the thoughts flash over her face. Hope followed by resignation. She didn't believe she had a choice. "You could stay here. Get a job."

"I thought of that, but I don't know anything except the army. That limits my choices."

"I have contacts. So does Nikolai. Henry. We could help you find a job."

"I don't spend much, but I still need somewhere to live if I stayed here. My father needs me. I don't have the option of walking away."

"We could pool our resources."

Mac frowned, slow to understand what Louie meant. "You mean live together."

"I mean get married. I don't want to live without you, Mac. I love you."

The contrast between Louie and David, her ex-fiancé had never seemed wider. David had walked away the moment he'd heard about her father. David hadn't loved her enough to overcome the obstacles. He'd never even considered trying to overcome them.

"But you're going to retire to a tropical beach somewhere. That's what you said." Her heart hammered, her breathing coming fast as she struggled to keep her feelings contained. Louie loved her.

"It won't be home without you, sweetheart. The last couple of months have shown me that." Louie reached out and brushed the hair from her face, the gesture so tender it made her heart stutter.

Could it be that easy? The answer? "So if I decide to go back to Iraq you're going too because you want to be with me?"

"Yes. I tried to find you after Fiji, and now that I've found you again, you're not escaping. Stay here with me in New Zealand."

"But what about my father? And what if you change your mind about a place at the beach?" David had.

"Your father can stay at the home. Together, we can swing the finances for as long as your father needs. Or if you want to have him with us, we'll work something out to make it happen."

Mac stared at Louie, searching his face for truth. "You mean it," she whispered finally. "No, I can't. I'd feel as if I was taking advantage of you. You might come to resent me." She hesitated before forging ahead. "One year before I met you in Fiji, I was engaged. My father was just starting to show symptoms of Alzheimer's. When he was diagnosed, David broke our engagement."

"He walked away?" The disbelief in Louie's voice made

her want to smile. The two men couldn't be more different.

"He wasn't happy about my choice of career either, even though he was army as well. He wanted me to retire." And had been very vocal about it, saying she was unfeminine.

Louie snorted. "The man was a fool. His loss. My gain." He grasped her hand and gently squeezed. "Mac, you don't need to do this alone. I know you love me. There won't be anything one-sided between us. Get a job if it makes you feel better. Either way, all I want is you. I don't want to lose you, especially not to a bomb or bullet in Iraq or in some other hot spot. But if that's where you're going, then I'm with you on the same plane."

Louie's words made her melt inside. She wanted to laugh, to dance and sing. A slow grin spread across her face, and she moved into his arms, pressing kisses over his face. The kisses went from sweet to demanding, hands stroking and soft sighs of pleasure. Louie's arms surrounded her, his scent and love. She felt love.

"You'll stay?"

"Are you sure?" she countered.

"Mac, I won't change my mind. I've loved you for a long time." He pushed inside her, the sense of completion bringing tears to her eyes.

"Good." And it was good. Great. She didn't want to

go back to Iraq. Some people might suggest she was frightened, her injury playing with her head. Mac knew better. It was because of Louie.

She stroked his cheek, felt the faint bristle of stubble along his jawline. The crinkle of smile lines around his eyes brought a return smile from her.

"I love you, Louie."

"I love you, Mac," he replied.

Mac paused, ran her hand down his shoulder and squeezed his butt cheek. "Joanna," she said.

He thrust, retreated and grinned. "Not every man gets two women in one package."

The piercing ache between her thighs deepened, and a groan built in her chest. "You're man enough to handle us both."

"I think so." Louie's chuckle contained a dose of sin. He rocked against her, the drag across her swollen clit shoving her into climax. She shuddered in his arms, ecstasy washing over her as she clung to him. Joanna "Mac" McGregor had found a man who wanted her as an equal, one who offered her a future full of happiness.

Mac wasn't fool enough to walk away from him again. This time was for keeps, and she couldn't be happier. No matter what the future brought, they'd face it.

Together.

THANK YOU FOR READING **Soldier With Benefits**, the second book in my *Military Men* series. Please turn the page to read an excerpt from **Safeguarding Sorrel**, book 3 in the *Military Men* series, and if you enjoyed this story, I hope you'll post a review at your favorite online store.

Shelley

EXCERPT—SAFEGUARDING SORREL

JAMES BARGED INTO THE Sloan police station, skirted the front desk, and strode down a dim-lit passage. He tapped on the second office door and opened it before anyone answered. "Luke, I might have found a way into the cult for you."

Luke Morgan, one of Sloan's cops and James's best friend removed his feet from the top of his desk and stood in one smooth motion. "Let's take this out of the station. I could do with a coffee."

"The cafe isn't private."

"We'll get coffee to go and wander down by the river. I think better on my feet."

Fifteen minutes later they strolled along the bank of the

203

river. Leaves crunched under their boots, sun streamed from overhead and a brisk wind rustled their hair.

"Talk," Luke ordered.

"One of the young cult girls approached me and Alice yesterday. She wants out of the cult."

"Why doesn't she just leave?"

"From what she told us she was born there. According to her once they're in, it's difficult to leave without resources. Any money they earn goes into a central pot. They're not encouraged to leave. She told us their long-term leader died six months ago. His son has taken over, and he has new ideas regarding the direction of the cult."

"Six months ago is about the time the farmers started complaining of missing cattle," Luke mused, interest sparking in his features.

"Yeah, the thought occurred."

"How is that going to help us get inside?"

"I thought Sorrel—that's the woman we met—might know of a way we can get someone inside, and once our man is in, she can help to smooth his path."

Luke nodded. "That's a possibility. Where can I meet her? When?"

James paused once they reached the bridge. He stared at a group of six ducks, quacking loud demands for food. "Do you have another plan?"

"No, other than going in with guns and shooting the weirdos. That's my stepmother's suggestion."

James spluttered out a laugh, the shake of his head flopping his dark hair over his eyes. He shoved it aside with a careless hand. "Hinekiri is a handful."

Luke snorted. "Where do you think my wife got it from? Janaya takes after her aunt. Yeah, I've thought about planting someone in the cult to spy for me. I have a guy, one of my cousin's friends, who needs something to keep him busy. He's a special services soldier on sick leave. My cousin reckoned he'd be perfect since he looks scruffy. Feeling sorry for himself, according to Louie."

"You've given this some thought. Sorrel told us she'd try to get away this afternoon after she delivers new supplies to their shop. She can't meet us in a public place. Any suggestions?"

"We can intercept her once she leaves the shop. If you see her beforehand, ask her," Luke said. "We'll meet her wherever she feels safest. I don't want to make her life any more difficult than it is now. She obviously feels she can't leave if she approached you in a clandestine manner. Ring me with details once you're set, and I'll be there. If I can't make the meeting for some reason, I'll send Janaya. Tell her that, will you?"

"Alice promised she'd meet her. Sorrel indicated a

meeting with a man would raise suspicion. One of the other cult women is bound to notice and report back to the men running the place."

"Makes sense. What's your impression of the woman?"

"Solemn and plain. Not much to look at, and a bit on the dumpy side."

"Yeah, but is she telling the truth? Could she be setting us up?"

James sipped his coffee. "No, I think she's genuine in wanting to get out. She was jumpy. Kept looking over her shoulder, and she doesn't think much of the new leader. You met him?"

"Yeah, he's charming but slimy with it. You know the sort. I can see him being controlling. What was Alice's take?"

"She wanted to help and was ready to take Sorrel home with us then. I'm not such a soft touch."

Luke shot him a swift glance. "She might be genuine."

"Maybe. Maybe not." He checked his watch. "I'd better go. We have a board meeting this afternoon. I'll call you the minute she gets in touch."

Does this undercover stint work?
Purchase Safeguarding Sorrel to find out.
(www.shelleymunro.com/books/safeguarding-sorrel)

ABOUT AUTHOR

USA Today bestselling author Shelley Munro lives in Auckland, the City of Sails, with her husband and a cheeky Jack Russell/mystery breed dog.

Typical New Zealanders, Shelley and her husband left home for their big OE soon after they married (translation of New Zealand speak - big overseas experience). A twelve-month-long adventure lengthened to six years of roaming the world. Enduring memories include being almost sat on by a mountain gorilla in Rwanda, lazing on white sandy beaches in India, whale watching in Alaska, searching for leprechauns in Ireland, and dealing with ghosts in an English pub.

While travel is still a big attraction, these days Shelley is most likely found in front of her computer following another love - that of writing stories of contemporary and paranormal romance and adventure. Other interests include watching rugby (strictly for research purposes), cycling, playing croquet and the ukelele, and curling up with an enjoyable book.

Visit Shelley at her Website
www.shelleymunro.com

Join Shelley's Newsletter
www.shelleymunro.com/newsletter

OTHER BOOKS BY SHELLEY

Fancy Free
Protection
Romp
Buzz
Festive

Friendship Chronicles
Secret Lovers
Reunited Lovers
Clandestine Lovers
Part-Time Lovers
Enemy Lovers
Maverick Lovers
Sports Lovers

Military Men
Innocent Next Door
Soldiers with Benefits
Safeguarding Sorrel
Stranded with Ella
Josh's Fake Fiancée
Operation Flower Petal
Protecting the Bride

Bundle
Military Men

Alien Encounter series
Janaya
Hinekiri
Alexandre

Bundle
Alien Encounter